CRONE of COCONUT COURT

DEAD & BREAKFAST #2

Gabrielle Keyes

Copyright © 2021 Gabrielle Keyes

CRONE OF COCONUT COURT

ASIN: B099QFPT2S (eBook Edition)
ISBN: 9798768037697 (Print Edition)

Characters and events in this book are fictitious. Any similarity to real persons, living or dead, is coincidental and not intended by author.

Printed and bound in the United States of America
First printing November 2021
Published by Alienhead Press
Miami, FL 33186

GABRIELLE KEYES

"Pretty, pretty, please, if you ever, ever feel,
Like you're nothing—you are perfect to me."

– P!NK

1

The cursor blinked.

I had only seconds to email the people at *Witch of Key Lime Lane* before my internet cut out. On tonight's episode, they'd flashed a help wanted ad for a temporary assistant job, but then my cable went out (on account of not paying my bill), so I had to act quickly.

Getting the job would mean moving all the way to Florida, a million miles from Iowa. Fine, maybe not a million, but a lot. I had no way of getting there after Nathan took our only car, and I also had no skills to speak of aside from being a mom to two beautiful girls and a wife to one dickhead. A dickhead who left me with $68 in our account.

But I still had a chance, didn't I?

Problem was…who did I think I was, applying for a position at a TV show while having no work experience? Aside from getting married at 22, having kids, and giving 22 years of my life to a man who, in the end, ran off with a woman *older* than me, I hadn't done jack shit with my life. That was my fault, I know. No one will ever convince me otherwise.

Over the years, I kept thinking, *Go back and finish college. Get a degree in something—anything—so you can stand on your own two feet IN CASE something goes wrong…*

But I never did.

Not because I wasn't smart—I was plenty smart—but because I'd applied what little savings Nathan had managed to earn toward the *girls'* college funds. Also because I'd trusted Nathan with every fiber of my being. From Day 1, he'd been my *everything*. He was my man. I'd believed he'd do right by me. In hindsight, that might not have been the smartest decision, but I'd had faith, good faith, that he would take care of me. Nathan never wanted me to work outside the home. He'd been raised to think that "the man" in a relationship should be the sole breadwinner, so for our whole marriage, he'd kept me in a holding pattern. Instead, I'd volunteered my ass off to pass the time.

PTA? Check.

Girl Scout Troop parent? Check.

Used bookstore clerk at our church? Check.

That one I did for me. What better way to spend my days than sitting in a store, surrounded by books that smelled like heaven, wiling away the hours, losing myself in worlds both fact and fiction? No, I didn't get paid, but the distraction was priceless. Besides, next door was *Betty's Fabric Barn*, an institution in my three-dog town of Melville, and anytime Betty had scraps of leftover fabric, she'd drop them in the donation box and let me rummage through it.

I got some nice pieces I used to make my girls pajamas when they were little. Sometimes I made matching PJs for their dolls as well. Hailey and Remy loved this until they got to be ten and twelve, when they started playing video games and hanging with middle school friends instead. I guess you could say I have sewing as a skill.

I once made a tablecloth for my pastor's daughter for her Christmas wedding using the good sewing machine Betty kept in the back. I'd sewn little holly berries and filigree into it, and the bride's grandmother raved about it for a week. It was the week after that wedding, when I came home early from volunteering, still on a high from everyone complimenting my tablecloth, that I found Nathan boinking a woman I'd never seen before in my life right on top of our microfleece SpongeBob blanket.

Would his deed have been easier to accept had I recognized the woman? I think so. I wouldn't have had to go down the rabbit hole of investigative work trying to figure out who she was. I would have been like, *Okay, Susy from church, I see you. You wanna bang my husband? I'm upset, but I'll get through this.*

Instead, I had no idea whose swinging boobs I was looking at. She was wearing a mask when I found her on all fours with her ass in the air. Not a BDSM mask either. Just a black mask. Like a COVID mask. Either that, or she had panties over her mouth. I don't know. I don't care. All I know is, for two years leading up to that night, I'd felt a cold distance creeping in between me and Nathan, so I was expecting it. Every time I went in for a hug, he'd pull away too quickly or say he had to work late.

So I ask you…

Who works "late" at a freakin' donut shop?

Then came my endless questions. Where did he meet her? Why did he bring her to *our* home, *our* bed, *our* SpongeBob blanket, the one place where I felt safe? Why not take her to a motel? I suspected why. He didn't have money for a hotel. He brought her to our home because he was a fucking cheapskate. A week later, he took off with half his stuff, leaving me $68 in our account and no idea what to do next.

He stopped responding to my texts. A myriad of thoughts keeps parading through my mind at all hours of the day, but I keep coming back to this one: *Thank God the girls are older.* I couldn't imagine the heartbreak they would've endured had he left when they were younger. Although, Hailey maybe not so much. As it was, she'd felt oppressed under Nathan's regime ("parenting style"), which included checking the girls' messages on their phones to make sure they weren't talking to boys (even after Hailey turned 18), removing the locks from their bedroom door, so they couldn't hide anything, and making them read the Bible every night.

Listen.

I was raised a good Christian girl, too, but nobody ever *made* me do those things. With Nathan, his rules were the law and nobody, not even I, could change or bend them. It was a bit much. The girls started hanging with me in the basement each night while I crocheted, in order to avoid reading the Bible, because I didn't force them. As a result, we formed a way stronger bond than they did with their father.

For the last six months, I'd been working at *Bill's Pharmacy* to make ends meet, but I needed more money. I needed a whole new life, but I had to start somewhere.

To Whom It May Concern, I typed. No—lame. I was applying for a position as a celebrity's assistant, not a banking job. They'd be looking for personality, bubbliness, talent—none of which I possessed. Nathan always said the girls' clothes I made looked like *Little House on the Prairie* rejects.

Ugh, so pointless. I stopped typing.

The only thing pointless is not trying, Katja, I could hear my Nana telling me. It'd been twenty years since I'd heard my grandmother's voice, but her memory always came right when I needed her. At least someone was looking out for me.

Brushing away tears, I straightened and tried again. "Dear Ms. Pulitzer..." I cracked a smile. On the show, Lily's wacky neighbor, Jeanine, always called her "Lilly Pulitzer" after the famous fabric designer.

"Thank you for offering the assistant position to your viewers," I read aloud as I typed. "One might wonder why you would do that, when you could simply hire a recent college graduate with experience in media, journalism, communications, or any skill set, for that matter. That is so not me..."

I reread what I had so far. Nobody would hire someone who didn't believe in themselves, so I hit the delete button on that last line before continuing.

"In fact, I thought my daughter might want to work for you since she loves your show, too, but she still has one more year to go before she graduates. Ms. Lily, I love my girls so much, I would do anything for them..."

Here I had to pause with fat tears perched on my lower lids. My girls were out in the world, nabbing their dreams, living their best lives, because of me. Because I'd saved the money. And that made me so proud. My girls were the one thing I'd done right. I'd given them opportunities. Choices. Unlike me, who'd never had.

I did that.

I'd had the wherewithal to set aside money every month since the girls were two years old. Why? Because I knew we wouldn't be able to pay for it otherwise.

Nathan felt that paying a college fund every month was a waste of perfectly good cash that could go toward "paying bills." He had no problem spending money on bait, extra beer, or Dungeons and Dragons, though.

Ms. Lily, I don't want to take up too much of your time, so I'll just answer the question your producers put up on the screen at the end of the show tonight—What makes YOU the perfect assistant for Lily Autumn?

I had just one shot to make them notice me, but what were the chances they'd choose me when I had zero qualifications? The more I sat there staring at the blinking cursor, the more I felt like an imposter.

Same chances as anybody else, Nanna said in my head.

She was right. There was nothing any college grad could do that I couldn't do better. I may not have had academic training, but I could learn anything. I had to stop feeling sorry for myself. I could do this. I wasn't worthless, even if Nathan had made me feel that way.

Ms. Lily, I'll be honest. I could tell you how I really need the job, how I'm a single mom, soon-to-be divorced, and my husband ran off with another woman. I know that would appeal to you after everything you went through, but that would be a cheap way of making you notice me, even if it's true.

The real answer is…

I heard the words in my head before I wrote them, but the ghost of Nathan's laughter rang in my ears. In spite of it, or maybe because of it, I wrote them anyway before I could change my mind: *I can do anything.*

I stared at the words.

They felt like a lie, but I knew them to be true.

That sounds stuck up, I know. I mean, who knows how to do "anything?" I can. I've just never been given the chance to prove myself. I know I can do whatever task you ask me to. If you hire me, I will show you what I'm made of. I can take notes for you, make your phone calls, clean your dishes, talk to your guests at the bed-and-breakfast. Sorry, DEAD & Breakfast. Ha, ha, I love that so much.

As a stay-at-home mom and empty-nester, I know I still have more of me to give. I'm only 44. All my life, I've felt like I'm on the verge of something big, something important, that never, ever comes. Then I was hit with the biggest blow of my life, and I thought, When will I get mine? When will I start living life? Not my husband's life, not my girls' life. For the first time, I'm alone with nowhere to go.

When I saw your job posting tonight, I thought, "That would be perfect for me. Go email Lily now!" So, this is me, seizing the moment, taking a risk. A huge step for me. I hope you choose me. If not because I'm desperate, then because I'm determined. Also, because I need to try Jeanine's key lime pie and because Skeleton Key looks like the most beautiful place on Earth.

Sincerely,
Katja Miller

Double-checking my spelling, I read the email one more time, cringed at half the stuff I wrote, then muttered a prayer. To God, the universe, or whoever was listening. At this point, it could be the Flying Spaghetti Monster—I wasn't picky. I sent off the email, heard the whoosh, then checked my Sent folder to confirm it was gone. Yep—my words were out in the world. Two seconds later, my internet went dead.

2

Flying into Miami International Airport was, by far, the most awe-inspiring experience of my life (besides having my daughters). Even from the air, I could tell the city sprawled with so much lush green, I thought I'd landed on a tropical island. Until this moment, the farthest from home I'd ever gone was to Aunt Clara's in Indianapolis. That was ten years ago.

At the airport, people whizzed by, speaking all sorts of different languages. Women toting designer bags wore tight clothes like Kim Kardashian or Housewives of Atlanta. My gosh, they were gorgeous. Could their curves be natural? I'd never seen booties so closely resembling the peach emoji.

Lugging my new carry-on (the network sent me money for new clothes and luggage), I bumped into a handsome silver fox wearing a suit and talking to himself. On second thought, he had AirPods in and was in the midst of a phone meeting.

"Perdona-blah-blah," he said something to me in Spanish, tapped my shoulder in kind gesture, and balanced both a sweater and hot coffee on his arm, like it wasn't 100 degrees outside.

"Oops. Excusez-moi," I said, miffed because where I came from, GQ cover models never touched my shoulder.

Standing by the luggage carousel was like a meeting at the United Nations. So many different colors of skin, hair, clothing styles, and languages again, I felt a little out of place. Miami was like another country within the US, and I hadn't even left the airport yet.

I allowed myself a triumphant smile.

I'd made it.

One month ago, the folks at *Witch of Key Lime Lane* called to tell me I'd gotten the assistant job. Lily Autumn had felt a connection with me. That night, sitting on the porch listening to the crickets, staring into my barren backyard, I broke into tears of shock. Would I have to tell Nathan? Would I have to share my paycheck with him? I know that sounds ridiculous; we were going through a divorce, after all, but I'd never been on my own before, not like this. Until the papers were signed, we were still technically married.

Weren't we?

Hell, no! Nana's voice yelled at me. *Don't you give that chump nothing!*

That night, I got my shit together and started packing. I wouldn't be leaving for another month, but I figured why not start the ball rolling, right? Even though I worried—*would they like me? Would they think they'd made a mistake, would they send me back in exchange for someone with more experience?*—I didn't let any of it stop me. One way or another, I would follow my instinct.

Now my instinct had led me here—to an airport 1,500 miles away from home. Victory #1.

Another gentle tap touched my shoulder. I turned, and wouldn't you know it? Another handsome man was standing there, except one I recognized. "Katja Miller?" He held a sign with my name on it.

I tripped over my foot and grabbed his arm for support. It was Captain Jax from the TV show, Lily's neighbor, the guy who gave boat rides to her guests and was basically head-over-heels in love with her. "Oh, hello. Yes, that's me." I tried to look as suave as one could while regaining balance on basic Keds.

Was it hot in here? I pulled my crumpled boarding pass from my carry-on and fanned myself.

Jax gave the cutest laugh. Gosh, his eyes really were that mossy green in real life, but there was also a twinkle to them that the camera didn't fully pick up. "I'm Jaxson Gomez. I'm here to whisk you away to Skeleton Key."

"Oh, that sounds lovely and creepy all at once."

"It is. You'll love it. Need help with your bags?"

"I only have one. The one your show paid for. I don't have luggage. What I mean is, I don't go anywhere. Wait, that's TMI. What I mean is, I wouldn't be able to afford a bag anyway, even if I did. The few times I've flown, I've always borrowed a bag."

Lord on a stick, what was wrong with me? Rambling like a madwoman? My cheeks flushed.

Captain Jax laughed again, a musical sound to match a charming smile. No wonder Lily Autumn kept him around. He probably thought I was a lame parrot when in real life, I was neither lame, talkative, nor a bird. "Right," he said. "Well, I can help carry your *one* bag. Is it that one?" He pointed to my suitcase, still sporting the manufacturer tag in case I needed to return it. Could I be any more embarrassing?

"Hmm, how did you guess?"

He checked the name on the tag, then heaved it off the carousel. "Just a hunch. Ready? Let's go."

I followed him down a hall, across a breezeway, and into the melting humidity of a Florida parking garage. "Holy moly, it's hotter than the devil's cinnamon buns."

Jax was even sweeter in real life than on TV because he laughed at everything I said, which Nathan never did. I found myself smiling a lot—a good thing. Already, this place was doing wonders for me.

We drove out of the airport, through gorgeous Miami, and onto the highway while making small talk about Melville, Iowa, how it was so different, how I'd never seen the ocean (or anywhere, for that matter), what my girls were up to. The more he asked me questions, the more inexperienced I felt, even for a woman my age. That made me sad, like I'd wasted a lot of time.

I got the sense that Jax felt sorry for me, but even though *I* felt sorry for me, too, I didn't want my new co-worker to feel that way about me, so I shut up and watched the scenery go by instead. But coming here *was* a big change. And I guess I *did* have a shitty backstory. I guess I just hadn't been as aware of it until I heard myself talking to Jax.

New starts called for new behavior. I wouldn't talk about Nathan anymore either, nor about never having a job before the pharmacy, nor about my boring life. The more we ventured toward the Florida Keys, the more excited I felt, the more my previous life melted away in the rearview mirror.

"So, the house you'll be staying at…" Jax said.

13

"I was wondering about that." No details were given during my interview, nor when I accepted the job. They could've put me in a coat closet, and I would've been happy.

"It's pretty old."

"Can't be older than the house I live in." Nathan's great-grandmother's 3-bedroom from 1931 was still in his family, so I knew I wouldn't be keeping it during the divorce.

"Yeah? Well, this one's got sweet potential," Jax said. "You'll like it. We're fixing it up. We've had workers come in daily to get it ready for you, but it still needs a lot of TLC. Today they're putting in a new circuit breaker box, so you'll be spending the night at Lily's."

"At the *Witch of Key Lime Lane* house?"

"The very one." Jax glanced at me over here, nearly falling out of the passenger seat with excitement. "You really are a fan, huh?"

"It's my favorite show. I love Lily. And you, of course. And Salty Sid, and Jeanine and Heloise. I'm all about creepy things, but my husband—my *ex*," I corrected, "never liked my interest in goth stuff."

I couldn't believe this was happening. I, Katja Miller, would be working for one of my role models? What had I done to deserve this? But I'd already broken my own rule of not talking about Nathan. Had to work on that.

"Well, for your first night, you get to be a guest at the witch's cottage," Jax said. "So, you'll be meeting everyone."

Ice dropped into my stomach. "Am I going to be on the show?" I hadn't considered being in front of the cameras. When they told me I'd be helping Lily, I assumed they'd meant behind the scenes.

"We're not taping at the moment. We're in between seasons. So, no film crew."

"Whew." My stomach unclenched itself. I was never one to like seeing myself in videos or selfies. "That's a relief. I'm not front-of-camera material."

Jax side-glanced me. "I wouldn't say that. Lily, Jeanine, Heloise, and I—we all got a pin-uppy vibe from you. With the right clothes, hair, makeup…hmm?"

Good Lord, Captain Jax was sizing me up? I turned my red face into the heated window. "I am somewhat of a closet ham." I laughed. "Do you know what I'm going to be helping Lily with? They didn't mention it during our phone call, and I was too excited about getting the job to ask."

"Other than helping get the new house ready, I'm not sure. But Lily will talk to you more about it. Never seen the ocean, huh? Well, how's that for culture shock?" He pointed.

My jaw nearly unhinged itself. There, to our left, was Her Royal Majesty, the Atlantic Ocean, in all her glistening, diamond-like glittery glory. I gasped, taking out my phone to take a picture, but my weak-ass battery died.

Better this way. I could take it all in. There'd be enough time for photos later anyway. "That is the most beautiful sight I've ever seen."

"Have to agree with you," Jax said. "I go out there every day, and I never get tired of it."

I wondered if I would be lucky enough to get to ride on *Sea Witch* myself. That was the name of Jax's boat, named after his mother who was some sort of ocean witch (supposedly). He talked about her in Episode 4, and it always made me wonder what he really meant. Because real witches—the fly on a broomstick kind— didn't exist. They made for good TV and a super-fun bed-and-breakfast theme, but ocean witches? Come on.

Gradually, the road gave way to one bridge after another, as we traveled through short islands where every car seemed to have a boat hitched to the back and every truck seemed to display red-and-white decals on the bumper about divers doing it deeper. I shook my head in awe at how different everything was.

When we turned off the highway and Jax steered into an old neighborhood filled with little Victorian-style houses, lots of white gravel rock in place of grass, rainbow flags, flamingo lawn ornaments, and mailboxes that looked like dolphins, I knew we'd arrived at the infamous Skeleton Key. It was interesting to see it all pieced together. In real life, the street looked older and less quaint than it did on TV. Lily Autumn's aunt, Sylvie, really had owned a rotting seaside cottage before Lily acquired it and turned it into a bed-and-breakfast.

But nothing could have prepared me for seeing the house, the actual house, before my very eyes. Before I knew it, we were there, pulling into the driveway. There it was—black and green with silver accents, elevated over a crawl space, lacy porch moldings, and charming shutters. A veritable witchy dollhouse. A gothic dream. If Lily Autumn came out to greet me in a pinup dress wearing an apron with her hair done up in Veronica Lake style, I would poop my pants. She didn't, but guess who did, meowing as the official greeter? While Jax fished my bag out of the trunk, the rockstar himself purred and rubbed his gorgeous white fur against my jeans, flashing his one-blue, one-green eyes at me.

"Is it really you? Bowie, I feel like I know you." I squatted to scratch the old kitty between the ears. He purred louder and pushed his head into my hands. For the hundredth time today, I couldn't believe my life.

"Watch out. He's a charmer." Jax shut the trunk. "Close your door at night, or you'll find a massive snow beast sleeping on your head."

I melted from the cuteness. "I wouldn't mind that." Honestly, it'd be nice to have a sweet, warm soul sharing a bed with me again, like my girls used to do when they were little. So many years ago. I swallowed a lump in my throat.

"There she is!"

What?

No way.

There she was—the goddess herself. The woman who'd brought herself back from humiliation after what her husband did to her, after the embarrassment of having her private life played out on TV for all to witness, after piecing herself back together and shoving the middle finger in her ex's face while having the last laugh.

But besides that…the owner of this beautiful establishment—Chef Lily Autumn.

"Doth my eyes deceive me?" I followed Jax up the steps, never taking my eyes off the lady herself. In shorts, white tank top, and flip-flops, no dramatic makeup, and a fresh sun-baked look, Miss Lily looked like anyone if they lived in the Florida islands. Except I could see the fine lines around her eyes now better than I could on TV, which gave her a wise, relatable appearance.

As I came up the last step, her arms opened wide, and with the sweetest of smiles, she said, "Oh, come here, you. You've come such a long way."

I stepped into her warm hug, and something inside of me broke down. Yes, ma'am, I had come a long way. Physically, but mentally, too. A long way indeed. And I desperately needed for another woman—someone my age, someone who looked like me, who'd been through what I'd been through this last year, who'd gotten hurt and humiliated yet come back from the grave—to understand that.

She seemed to recognize that and hugged me for however long that took, because time stood still, to be honest. At the moment, she wasn't a celebrity chef on the *Cooking Network*, nor a respected restauranteur, business-owner, or someone I looked up to with all my soul. She was just Lily.

"Thank you." I choked back tears. "I will do whatever you need me to do, Ms. Lily. I'm at your service."

"Just Lily, love. Come inside for some pie."

"Key lime pie?" My heart exploded into citrusy green hearts.

She smiled—a lovely, warm smile that lit up her golden honey eyes. "Is there any other kind?"

3

How many people could say they'd stayed at the *Witch of Key Lime Lane* house, otherwise known as *Sylvie & Lily's Dead & Breakfast*? From one day to the next, I'd gone from sad, lonely divorcée to luckiest girl in the world. My new life was shaping up already, on account of pure location, and I hadn't even been here an hour.

After quick chit chat over the tangiest, creamiest, best key lime pie I'd ever tasted (fair enough, the only key lime pie I'd ever tasted), Lily showed me to the guest room she called "Luna's Lair" after the ghost cat she talked about on the show a lot.

"This is where I first watched her disappear before my very eyes." She stared and pointed to the closet. "Right there. She went—*flit*—underneath a desk we used to have in there."

I nodded contemplatively.

I'd never seen a ghost cat, or any ghost, before, but *Witch* viewers claimed to see Luna quite often. Before my internet cut out, I used to read posts by members of her Facebook community page, claiming to see Luna lurking behind Lily. They'd share screenshots or circle some muddy smudge on the floor they thought might resemble a gray cat with golden eyes. I'd seen the vintage black-and-white photograph of Luna in front of this house when it used to belong to the famous rumrunner, Annie Jackson, however, so if I did see her ghost, I'd know who to look for.

Look, it wasn't that I didn't believe in spooks or witches—it was that I'd never seen any myself. If humans were meant to see them, wouldn't they be out in the open? Why would we have to try and prove their existence? My Nana talked to me all the time, but that was more my spirited imagination than ghosts, I thought. I just missed her so much, and the brain is capable of seeing what it wants to see, you know?

But I didn't want to offend Lily, so I just said, "That must've been amazing to witness."

"Oh, it was," she said. "When you first realize what you're seeing, your brain doesn't know how to process it. It's quite an experience. You'll see." She gave a little laugh.

"I will?"

"If you stay in Skeleton Key long enough? Yep." She tapped the door frame. "Anyway, I'll let you get settled in. When you're ready, find me downstairs, and I'll walk you to the Berry House."

"Is that…?"

"Where you'll be staying." She smiled and closed the door gently, leaving me alone in the beautiful guest room decorated with all sizes and shapes of stars, moons, and glowing golden suns on rich purple walls, potted palms in each corner. The backside of the door boasted a painting of Luna on the bottom edge, so when you opened and closed the door, she appeared then disappeared.

I giggled. "I see what you did there, Lily."

A coffin-shaped, built-in shelf contained large, chunky crystals, geodes, and glass spheres with a resin sculpture of a sexy witch riding a black cat like a cowboy, and the desk next to it had a flip-top lid, more like a vanity. I wondered if that had been the desk inside the closet.

Inside were different sets of Tarot cards. I touched nothing, only observed and marveled. All stuff I'd seen on ten episodes of Season 1. Throwing my bag onto the bed, I lay down next to it and stared at the ceiling fan with the wide, brown, tropical designed paddles.

Well. Here I was.

After plugging in my phone, I selected the few photos I'd taken so far and sent them off to the girls. *Finally made it!*

Yay! Have you met Lily yet? Is she nice? Hailey replied right away.

Yes, very. I'll talk to you soon.

With a huge sigh, I spread out on the bed and was about to drift off into a light nap when my phone dinged. Probably my other girl, but when I looked, it was Nathan.

Are you home? Need to pass by and get a few things.

What the hell? I hadn't heard from him in seven months, and now suddenly, he wanted to drop by? What were the chances? I stared at the screen, my jaw slack, hands trembling so hard, the phone slipped from my grip and hit the bedspread.

Other than the girls and my boss, Bill of *Bill's Pharmacy*, I hadn't told anyone I was coming down to Florida, and I was pretty sure Nathan hadn't talked to either Hailey or Remy. The day he left, he stopped communicating with me, the girls, and even his extended family, and even if he had gotten in touch with the girls, they wouldn't disclose my location without talking to me first. They'd always been mama's girls.

Picking up the phone again, I tried typing with shaky fingers. *No, I'm not. Sorry.* There, let him wonder where I was. That would be fine for now, but what if he tried going by the house and found it sitting in the dark, making him wonder where I'd gone?

It don't matter what he thinks, baby, I could hear my Nana saying. *He can go boil his head in cabbage stew for all we care.*

That was all good and fine for my grandmother to say. She never took shit from nobody, but she also never knew Nathan well. How ornery he could get. I'd kept that part a secret from her. She never liked the way he controlled me and the girls, but she never knew his darker, aggressive side, and if Nathan knew I'd hopped off and gone to Florida, he'd be mad as hell.

Did it matter? What he thought?

Weren't we almost divorced?

Yes, the agreement just needed his signature, so then what did I care?

It made sense when other people told me to forget Nathan. Even Betty from *Betty's Fabrics*, a traditional, churchgoing old woman, had let loose her opinion of Nathan once or twice, so if she could send Nathan to hell in her mind, why couldn't I?

'Cause he still got a hold on you, Nana said.

Yeah. And I had to let that go.

What time you be home? Nathan texted.

My heart pounded like a trapped rat in a cage. Why was I so scared of him? Because if I knew Nathan, he didn't *just* want to know what time I'd be home; he also wanted to know where I'd gone, who I was with, and if I was with any man. As if he had any right to know.

I didn't respond. Instead, I stood to shake him off, unpacked a few things, and removed from my suitcase the one thing I shouldn't have brought to Skeleton Key—our SpongeBob blanket. Yes, it was a traumatic reminder of what he'd done, but it also gave me some sort of dominion over him. The blanket was mine now, and he couldn't take it from me.

I changed into shorts and a tank top (when in Rome), then headed downstairs—without my phone. It was a start.

I stood staring up at a dilapidated, old house on the beach, one street down from Key Lime Lane. 111 Coconut Court was the address, an exotic sounding name, except the place looked less coco-nutty and more coco-rotty. Just seeing the house's leaning front porch made me weepy, but maybe that was the ninety-five-degree sweat.

"I just bought it," Lily said next to me, proudly. "The previous owners kept it as a winter home, but they hadn't been down in the Keys for a few years, due to their advancing age, so I made an offer."

"And they took it, obviously."

"Yes, but not at first. They held on for a few months. People here do that. These old houses are full of history, like mine with the distillery."

"I love the story of the distillery!" I clapped. "So, this house was a distillery, too?"

"No, this one was the theater, I think."

"Doesn't look like a theater."

"The actual theater burned down. This was the connecting house. I think. In any case, the island's first residents were considered sketchy people at the time, so I'm sure it was used for something illegal. In those days, the Keys were the last resort, the last depot, the end of the world for someone in the 1920s. People came down here to hide from the law. Or from life."

"Are you going to live in it?" I asked.

"No, I have my house. Here's the thing…" In the orange glow of late afternoon, she shielded her honey eyes, and I got a full picture of just how beautiful she was. Older than me by two or three years, Lily was in great, middle-aged shape with radiant skin and face angles made for television. "I might want to turn it into another *Dead & Breakfast*."

"Oh?" I sounded less excited than I'd hoped to convey. "I mean, no offense, but it looks like someone let the air out of its tires."

She laughed. "I know, but that's how my aunt's house—my house—looked, too, when I first arrived. Depending on its condition after a few inspections, I'll decide whether to renovate or flip it."

"Is that what you need my help with?" I asked.

"Yes. I need help cleaning the place out. There's a literal ton of boxes that need going through, stuff the previous owners left behind."

"Why didn't they take their belongings?"

"They took furniture but left a bunch of trunks and boxes. Stuff they said they didn't need, but I heard from Nanette, their neighbor over there…" She pointed to a tidy modern, one-story house behind us. "That they never came back after their last visit because they got spooked."

"Weird."

"Maybe, maybe not. The truth is, snowbirds who buy these as second homes sometimes neglect them." Lily stared wistfully at the Berry house. "Anyway, it all needs to go, but I'm also hoping there might be some good finds in there I can use."

"I'm all about good finds!" I said. "So, if the Berrys don't want the stuff, and I find stuff you don't want either, then I just toss it?"

"Oh, the previous owners weren't the Berrys."

"Who are the Berrys then?"

"Just one Berry—Josephine. The original owner. It's known as the Berry House, even though she hasn't lived here in a hundred years."

"So, the previous owners are…"

"The Fletchers. They owned the house for about twenty years. Someone else owned it twenty years before that, and someone else twenty years before that. It hasn't stayed in one family for longer than that."

"Like my ex's house," I said.

"Oh, it's a family home?"

I nodded. "Probably why I'll be homeless after the divorce is over."

"Don't say that," Lily said with a sad smile. "Everything will turn out for you. Believe me, it will."

I nodded. I knew she was right. Things turned out well for her, but then again, Lily probably had a savings during her divorce, a house she could sell, a restaurant in her name, whereas I had nothing in mine. Zero. Zilch. If I had to move into a tiny apartment in Melville when this was all over, that would be fine, but I'd miss the house I'd called home for twenty-two years.

"Anyway, do you think a house that's been around for a hundred years might have a cool heirloom here or there?" I asked.

"I doubt it, but I am hoping for a few interesting pieces I can possibly use as décor. I don't expect more than that." The light in her eyes took over her soul, and I saw what Lily Autumn was passionate about. Not cooking, though I was sure she was passionate about cooking, too—but discovery.

Treasure.

Secrets.

The sort of stuff I only read about in books.

She opened the front door using a key that hung from a foam sandal keychain. "Can you blame me for hoping? After the stuff I found in my own house?" She smiled.

"No, ma'am, I cannot. Would you be adding this bed-and-breakfast to the show if you decided to convert it?"

Her side-glance swelled with mischief. "I knew I liked you the moment I read your letter, Katja. It was your honesty, your transparency, that really got me."

"Aw, shucks."

"No, really. It's quite refreshing. Honesty is a big deal to me. But to answer your question—yes, that would be the ultimate goal—a Season Two. Come, let me show you around."

So, my job was to sift through this old house for two months to see what I could find. I could do that. I needed the space from Melville anyway, the girls were at school, and I had no home—not anymore. I decided what she should keep and what she should toss, and if I found any vintage antiques, I was to set those aside. But when the job was done, then what?

Where would I go?

You don't have to decide right now, Nana told me.

I walked into the house, and my nose began to twitch. Okay, it wasn't that bad. It wasn't falling-apart old. It was simply old-people old. Now, at my age, I had no business calling other people old, but the interior of this house made me feel like a teenager cringing at her grandparents' house.

Lily showed me the tiny, outdated kitchen in bright yellow, the living room covered in tacky, newborn poop-colored wallpaper with vertical stripes and blue, pink, and white roses, a small, stuffy dining room with nasty blue carpet, and a set of carpet-covered stairs leading into the gloom.

"What are you thinking right now?" Lily asked me.

"That it's old but it's a house? A place to live? That I'm incredibly grateful you're giving me a job…"

"I am, but you have to be certain you want to work here. I know it's a lot. There's a shit-ton to sort through, the A/C isn't working, it's hot outside, but you said you were up for the challenge."

"I am."

"Even after what you've seen so far?"

"Yes, ma'am, what's so bad about it?"

She studied my face. Maybe she thought it was an awful place, but I didn't think so. Beggars couldn't be choosers, and a house was a house. A job was a job. "You sparked my interest when you said you could do anything, Katja, so I guess I'm curious to see what that might entail."

"Well, Ms. Lily, I can clean the hell out of a dirty old house, for starters. I can rip this wallpaper out like it's a wax strip, and I can even sketch designs for you."

"Oh? Do tell."

"Yeah, you know, ideas on what the house could look like with a complete makeover, but still in tune with your current witchy theme. Heck, I can even sew you some new curtains if you find me a sewing machine. I mean, I'm known as Queen of the Sewing Machine back where I live."

She chuckled. "For real?"

"No." My own confidence felt fake but justified, and I knew if I stood here talking long enough, she would see right through me. "But seriously, I would love to stay and help you."

"Let's go upstairs then."

"Why, what's upstairs?"

"The trunks."

"The trunks?" I stammered.

"Yes. Follow me."

4

"According to Nanette," Lily explained, "the last owners were scared of the trunks."

"Which trunks?"

"The ones I'm about to show you."

Sounded ominous. "Are they filled with dead bodies, or something?"

She giggled. "No, but apparently, they have a mind of their own."

Ah, she meant more haunted stuff. If that was the case, I wouldn't be scared. You had to believe in that sort of thing in order to be scared.

Upstairs was in slightly better condition. At least the floors seemed to be pine or other original wood, sans yucky carpeting, and the walls were painted a relatively modern light blue. The stairs ascended in a dizzying square pattern, so at the top, I was able to look down the center well.

Though the home was Victorian-style from the early 1900s, and somewhat small, like Ms. Lily's one street over, its architecture was entirely different than *Sylvie & Lily's Dead & Breakfast*. It was prettier, more ornate. It hadn't looked like much from the outside or downstairs, but up here, I saw its dollhouse-like potential.

She led me into a large, empty room that faced the beach with angled ceilings and dirty, scuffed wainscoting. The windows were open, letting in hot, salty breezes that could scrub a soul straight clean. A queen-sized IKEA-style bed had just been built, judging from the wordless instructions still on the floor.

"This used to be their bedroom." Lily twirled. "We put that in for you. Temporarily. Until we get the place furnished. I apologize if it's dinky."

"Dinky?" I glanced at the bed and the spacious master bedroom. "This whole room is nearly bigger than my house back home."

"Good. I'd keep the windows open at night, if I were you, so you can get the ocean breezes until we replace the A/C units with central A/C. For now, they should get the unit up and running in the meantime."

"Not a problem."

"And over here…" She moved toward a walk-in closet and opened its door wide for me to peek inside. Except for two large leather trunks, it was empty. "Are two of the trunks. There's two more in the other room. I'll show you."

"So those belonged to the previous owners?"

"No. Apparently, they've been here since the original owner."

"And nobody takes them when they move out?"

She shrugged. "Guess not. Don't know why. Maybe they're too heavy or cumbersome. Anyway, they said to keep whatever we wanted and throw away the rest."

"What's so scary about them?" I asked. They looked like regular trunks to me.

Lily raised an eyebrow. "It's always something with them. We try opening them with a key, and they stay stuck. Other times, we find them open. At the moment, they seem to want to be locked."

"So, you're telling me that these trunks sometimes open by themselves?"

She nodded. "I know it sounds odd, but trust me, that's the most dangerous thing that's happened so far. Nobody's ever been hurt in this house."

At that very moment, something snapped and fell in the hallway. Both Lily and I stuck our heads out to see what might've made the noise, but we saw nothing. We exchanged looks and laughed.

"Like I was saying," Lily said. "Idiosyncrasies…"

"You've used that word on the show before."

"Yes, because there's no other way to describe these homes. The houses on Skeleton Key have a life of their own. They've been around longer than you and I put together, Katja. They'll let you know when they're ready for new people. This one, so far, hasn't seemed ready."

I scratched my head. How could a house be ready for new people? A house was just walls, floors, wooden beams, stucco, wallpaper, and paint. Sure, people made it a home through their personality and style, but it seemed more likely to me that the trunks just got stuck sometimes. They were old, they got rusty, and salty, humid air made them cranky.

A muffled, buzzing sound cut through the quiet. She glanced at her phone. "I have to take this." Lily moved to the large window and stared out at the dusky tangerine sky. "Mm-hmm, yes. Yes, send him over...oh, okay. I'll be there in a minute." She hung up and turned to me. "I have to get back to the house. Forgot to send a recorded interview for a magazine. Is it okay if I leave you here to look around? And if you have any questions, you can call me or come get me."

"I left my phone and stuff at your place. I'll come get it all in a minute. Didn't feel like reading my texts." I sighed.

"Oh, no. Everything okay?" She lifted an eyebrow.

"My ex, or soon-to-be anyway, decided after seven months to drop by the house without warning, and now he'll know I'm not there."

"Why should he know if you're there?"

It was such a valid question, one for which I had no answer. My silence must've told her everything she needed to know.

"Oh, boy," she groaned. "I know that feeling all too well. I hope you told him to mind his own beeswax. What you do is no longer his concern."

"I did, but you don't know Nathan. He thinks he owns me. I know that's my fault for letting him believe that for so long. Not anymore, though."

She nodded slowly. "Yes. You have to stop answering his texts, first of all."

"That's why I left my phone."

"Do you think he will be an issue while you're here?" she asked. Something about her question sent a shiver of panic through me.

33

Wait, would Nathan try and find me? If he did, would he make a scene or cause problems for Lily? On one hand, I hoped he'd be too preoccupied with his face-panty-wearing girlfriend to care about anything I did anymore, but on the other, Nathan never could stand the fact that I might be living my life without him.

"He doesn't know where I am, and I intend to keep it that way. Sorry if all that was TMI."

"No worries. You'll soon discover that your TMI becomes everybody's TMI on this island. I learned that within a day, coming from the big city." She moved into the hallway and admired the high ceiling.

"I come from a small town," I said. "I know how that works. In fact, I'm surprised more people haven't dropped by to get the scoop on my life yet. It's been practically twenty-four hours since I arrived."

"I told them to give you space." She winked. "Anyway, sorry to run off. The fridge is fully stocked, there's electricity, there's wine. Make yourself at home. Take a walk on the beach or sit on the nice big patio. I'll be back soon."

"Sounds good."

She skittered off, leaving me alone in the big ol' house. I walked through the rooms, grazing my fingers over walls and banisters, checking out the other two locked trunks, plus a Great Wall of Boxes in one of the other two bedrooms, about twenty or so.

"Guess we'll be getting to know each other soon enough," I whispered.

A breeze blew through the bedroom window, and in the distance, the soft sound of a bell complemented the cry of gulls and lapping of waves. I was in Florida. I never would've imagined myself here, but then again, I never would've imagined my life torn apart either. It felt odd to be without my girls or even Nathan. I felt sad, lonely, and incomplete, and standing in this stranger's house, committing myself to cleaning it felt alien.

I inhaled a deep breath through my nose and let it out slow. The bell grew louder, as whoever was ringing it apparently got closer. I headed downstairs, cutting through the living room where I noticed a circular buzzsaw and toolbox neatly put away together in one corner. Workers had already started repairing the house. Good thing, because the home had such potential.

I stepped onto a gorgeous back patio with shiny, glazed terra cotta tiles and slowly-spinning ceiling fan paddles. Lily was right, this was a nice place to hang out and watch the ocean, and I was getting paid to be in Heaven! A little white boat slowly bobbed in on the waves, cutting through seaweed, with an older man wearing a baseball cap at the helm.

I knew him immediately from the TV show. He was real!

"Ahoy!" Salty Sid waved.

I waved back. "Ahoy!" There he was! In person!

"You Lily's new girl?" he asked.

"Yes, Katja." I stepped onto the white sands for the first time and walked up to the famous fisherman on Lily's show, whose baseball cap today read: *Booty Hunter*. Seeing he'd opened a white cooler to show off his goods, I peeked in. "What you got there?"

"Yellowtail, dolphinfish, a few lobster, mussels…what you got a hankering for?"

My genuine smile at meeting Sid melted away. "Oh, I can't buy anything today. Sorry. Maybe after my first paycheck."

"I didn't ask how much money had. I asked what you got a hankering for?" He winked a crinkly blue eye. "On me."

"Oh, I couldn't do that to you."

"Yes, you can. The network people give me a paycheck, too. Go make yourself a nice welcome dinner with some fresh catch. Name is Sid, by the way. They call me Salty Sid." He stretched out his hand, which I took and shook heartily.

"I know. I love seeing you on *Witch of Key Lime Lane.* You're so good to Lily; I had to see you to believe you're real."

"Oh, I'm real, honey. Sorry, didn't mean to call you honey. I know that's offensive these days. I don't look down on you. In fact, I admire the way you've handled all the crap-crapola that's come your way this last year. 'Sides, 'Katja' is so much prettier than 'honey.' Crap, there I go again, devaluing you by saying your name is pretty instead of 'intelligent' or 'hardworking.'"

Sid was the real deal. I giggled. "It's fine. Wait, you know about my life the last year?"

"Course I do. Helped Lily choose you from over two thousand applicants. For a whole week, we sat in her back patio and reviewed the applications and the videos y'all sent."

"Two thousand?"

"Something like that. Yep. Heloise, Jax, and Jeanine helped, too. Anyhoo, that ex of yours sure got some balls bringing his floozy into the house the way he

36

did." Salty Sid shook his head in complete non-acting sympathy.

I'd forgotten that I'd told that story in my video segment, Phase 2 of the application process, after they'd narrowed down the prospective hires. Dumb of me to think only Lily would watch it. I should've known the "producers and crew" would also mean the show's supporting cast.

"I'm so embarrassed." I covered my face.

"Why?" Sid bristled. "No way, fillet. Nothing to be embarrassed about. Wasn't your fault. They don't make men anymore the way they used to. That's the problem, see. Someone ought to whip that boy. Yellowtail?" He held up a pretty silver-yellow fish. "Don't need much. A little lemon and garlic, and you're good to go."

"Sure, I…that would be amazing. Thank you," I said, still coming to terms with the fact that Salty Sid knew my shit. However, the sooner we could get it out of the way that my philandering husband left me with $68 and skedaddled out of town, the sooner we could move on.

"You got yourself the Berry House there, didn't ya?" With his chin, he pointed at the cracked and peeling building behind me. From the back, its shape was gorgeous, tall and narrow and poetic, leaning up against the clouds like that. Vibrant shades of orange, purple, and yellow in the background. Absolutely stunning sky.

"That's what I'm told. It needs a little love on the outside. Inside does too, but I was surprised by how lovely the upstairs is."

"Well, it *was* lived in until recent years. Good thing the men have started coming out to fix things up. Knowing Ms. Autumn, she'll have the place looking pristine in no time."

"To sell or to keep?" I asked, just to see what Sid would say, in case he had insider information. Trick I learned in Melville.

"Not sure, though how cool would it be for Lily to own both the island distillery *and* the burlesque theater?"

"That was crazy when she told me that, too. I have a hard time imagining this place as an auditorium back in the day, and right on the sand, too."

"Yeppers, but it wasn't that big, I don't think. Burlesque theaters were pretty small. They weren't showing no operas, if you know what I mean." Sid chuckled.

"Oh, Sid." I laughed, too.

"Josephine Berry ran the place way back when, both as its owner and operator but also its star performer. A real looker, if you ask me, but that was before I was born, even."

"Oh, wow. Did she know Annie Jackson?"

"I think she lived a bit before Annie's time. Look it up. Info's online. By the way, I didn't mean anything by it when I said she was a real looker. Smart businesswoman, too, that one was. Too bad a fire took down her theater."

"That's horrible."

"Indeedly-dee. To this day, no one knows how it happened. The official reported cause was electrical fire by hurricane, but…I always wondered if it was more."

"Interesting. You'll have to tell me more when—"

"See, if you go upstairs into one of the bedrooms, you'll notice the wall where the main house used to connect to the theater balcony. It's not a load-bearing wall, more of an interior wall that was covered by stucco on the outside to reinforce it, and you can sort of see the warped lines connecting to the closet, and…"

Sid prattled on, but the truth was I was feeling hot as a whore in church standing out here under the sun, and I hadn't intended to get a whole architectural lesson on Day One.

"…so why would there be two areas that look affected by fire if it was caused by hurricane. Know what I mean?"

This sounded interesting as all heck, but I was starving, needed to get my stuff from Lily's, and would have a couple months to get the scoop. "Yeah, totally see what you're saying. Hey, maybe next time you come by, you can tell me your theories on it. Sound good?" I smiled, so Sid wouldn't think I was blowing him off.

"Ooo, be careful, you. Invite this old man over and he'll never stop talking. Alright, Ms. Katja, welcome to Skeleton Key where the sunsets are forever, the mojitos flow, and the magic is real. Enjoy the yellowtail." Twinkly-eyed Sid whistled a pirate-like tune, pushed his boat back onto the waves, and continued on his course down the shore.

My life, despite the crapola, was amazing.

5

Look, the bed wasn't the most comfortable in the world, but did I care? No, because I woke up the next morning to a full Atlantic Ocean sunrise gloriously beaming straight through the Berry House's master bedroom window.

I live here now, I thought in awe. *For the time being, anyway. I may not own this house, but I have it all to myself, and I'm getting paid in actual dollars to organize it.*

Flinging aside the fluffy white comforter, I stretched, about to jump in the shower, when other truths jammed their way into my memory, elbowing, kicking and screaming.

You have no life. Your husband left you. He ran off with another woman, took all the money you had as a couple, and you don't have any skills. Remember, Katja, my brain sneered, *you've been hired to clean a ratty old house, a skill anybody with half a brain can do. Lily only hired you because she pitied you.*

"Shut up," I groused, dropping my feet to the floor and stumbling into a bathroom filled with cracked

GABRIELLE KEYES

subway tiles and peeled-away caulking that revealed
moldy edges and corners.

Even if that nasty voice in my head was right, I
was here when I could've been home, cashiering at a
pharmacy, seeing the same people, day in, day out. It
may have been pure, dumb luck that had gotten me here,
but it was luck I hadn't had a couple of months ago.

Tell the voice to shut up, Nana told me. *Remember
the song…*

My grandmother and I didn't live in the same
town, so we relied on phone conversations and email to
talk, exchange jokes, and tell each other about our day.
When Pink's song, *Fucking Perfect,* came out, Hailey was
little and used to love singing it. Every time Nana was on
the phone, she'd ask to hear Hailey belt it, which she
would, loudly and proudly. When she was done, she'd
run off to play, and Nana would tell me, *She's right, you
know. If you ever feel like you're nothing…you're
perfect…to me.*

I let the shower run over me, washing away the
negative self-talk. *I'm trying, Nana. I'm trying.*

That voice had always been my toughest battle.
All my life I'd struggled with it and being married to
Nathan hadn't made it any better. At first, I thought he'd
make me better as a person. Being with a man in charge
would teach me how to be assertive, would make me
proud, more confident, but as time wore on, Nathan
stole every little victory from me. If someone praised any
clothing I'd made, he had to say that the pattern was
easy. Or the fabric was what made the tablecloth look
good. Or the person wearing it. Anything would look
amazing on two little girls.

41

Sure, my cherub-cheeked daughters could've made anything look cute when they were babies (even now), but screw you, Nathan, I'd also sewn them cute pajamas, damn it. I'd done it—me. Yet I never stood up for myself and I hated myself for that. I was always so scared of the conflict and argument that would surely ensue, because Nathan loved to argue until he'd proven himself right or wore you down, whichever came first.

But today was a new day, and I wasn't going to let him ruin it. Not when a gorgeous beach stretched outside my window, and the view of the ocean was mine, all mine. Still, I couldn't help it and checked my phone, seeing no less than fifteen text messages from him, demanding to know where I was. I reveled in knowing my daughters hadn't let the cat out of the bag, otherwise he wouldn't have been still asking at 3:17 AM, the time of his last text.

I let out a breath, tightened the towel around my hair, and was about to dry my legs, when I heard a creak. From where in the house, I had no idea. I wasn't yet familiar with the sounds of this house and felt nervous even stepping one foot into the hallway.

"Hello?"

A soft shuffle against either floorboard or other surface alerted me to the south-facing bedroom, the one with the ridiculous amount of boxes waiting for me to go through them—Mount Boxmore. Each damp footstep against the wood floor created a new creak. With my heart thumping in my ears, it was hard to focus my hearing. I stopped in the hallway, dust motes swirling in the horizontal swags of morning light, hoping to God that I was alone.

I waited for the noise.

In the distance came boat horns and the caw of a seagull. I was about to retreat, dismiss the noise off to the house settling when I heard the shuffle again. I peeked into the room, a high vibrational energy filling my ears, my brain fully expecting to see a person standing there, when…I saw no one. Literally no one.

"Dear Lord…" I whispered, about to turn around when the soft shuffling happened again, and this time, a flash of bright green caught my eye. My gaze snapped to the left, where I saw it—a long, bright, thorny, spiky, super bright lime green mini dinosaur on top of one of the boxes near the open window. "Jesus H. Christ."

I fell to the floor, grasping my heart, wanting to scream but at the same time realizing how incredibly stupid that would be. *It's an iguana. Of course, it's an iguana. I'm in Florida, the windows are open, it's hot, it's summer, and this is a tropical island.* But were iguanas safe to have around? Did they bite? Should I call Wildlife & Services? What did one do when faced with an enormous lizard wearing a dark green and yellow mohawk?

The iguana looked just as surprised to see me as I was to see it, him, her—whoever. His eyeball spun, cocked, reversed, stared at me, as I slowly stood to see him more closely. "You…" I scolded the lizard. "Scared me. How dare you? You know I'm new here."

Let's just call him Iggy. Iggy the Iguana shifted positions, skittered back, and tried to hide behind a box behind him all while his little claws scraped the cardboard box, creating the shuffling sound I kept hearing. He looked ready to run if I got any closer. If iguanas could speak, this one would surely say, *Don't come any closer, lady. I mean it. Stay where you are.*

"I assume, under good faith, that you are not here to hurt me," I told Iggy. "Only that you saw an open window, and like any good reptile, decided to escape the morning breeze by entering a warm room."

Iggy's eyeball swiveled.

"Then you may stay." I slowly backed out until I reached the door, ready to return to my room and get dressed when I noticed something else. Something I hadn't seen until now, though for all I knew, could've been this way since last night. A trunk was open.

I was pretty, fairly, positively sure it had not been open yesterday when Lily was here, after she left, even. I'd walked through this room and seen that trunk, plus the one next to it, were closed. Were they sealed? Or locked? I had no idea. I hadn't tried opening them at the time, but at this very moment in time, it was open— wide open. Lid yawning all the way up.

With one eye on Iggy and one eye on the mysterious trunk, I quietly chose the trunk to inspect and peek inside. Colors and textures exploded into view— magenta velvet, white lace, black netting, turquoise pom poms, peacock feathers, cow pelts, sequins and glittery fabrics, canvas, and linen. I reached in and plucked out a few items—a black feather boa, a white tablecloth, a red garter with black lace border, a cowboy vest, a cowboy hat, and more. Costumes. Accessories. Setting them on the edge of the trunk so I could keep pulling out items, I did my best to reach the bottom where I felt around with my fingers until the tips touched something hard and smooth.

Curling my nail around a hard, smooth loop, I pulled out a teacup. Knowing nothing about teacups or porcelain, whether they were fake or real china, all I knew was that it was beautiful with its pink flowery pattern and gold trim on the brim and handle. I pulled out another cup and another, along with tiny saucers, and eventually sat on the floor with the trunk's booty laid out around me.

From across the room, Iggy closed his eyes, apparently comfortable enough with me to withdraw his caution, as he basked in the sun coming in at a sharp angle. How long had this stuff been here? Since the theater days? Or did this belong to the previous owners, who happened to have grandchildren who liked to play dress-up? What were the chances that any of the contents might be a hundred years old?

I suddenly remembered my purpose for being here—to decide what should stay and what should go. Would Lily want a bunch of old costumes? Probably not. It didn't fit the theme of her Dead-and-Breakfast, so unless she wanted to open a daycare or community theater, this would probably all get donated. A shame, because back home, I'd keep some of this stuff to play around with. But I wasn't home—I was here on a mission, and Lily Autumn was depending on me to make decisions on her behalf while she was busy with work.

It was time to get dressed, head downstairs, and see what breakfast I could whip up. I was about to turn back into the bedroom when I heard yet another noise downstairs, the sound of an actual door opening and closing. "Seriously? I can't..." My heart leaped into my throat. Was the house open to anyone, or would I have privacy while here?

I stood at the railing, looking down the square stairwell. "Hello?" I called.

A moment later, a voice very much not Lily's, very deep and resonant, replied. "Hello?"

Immediately, internal alarms went off in my body. My brain thought Nathan, and I started to sweat all over again. He'd found me and was about to give me the third degree. Whether I liked it or not, we were still married, and I needed to obey him. He would kill me for leaving Melville.

Fuck that, Nana's voice said.

"I agree," I muttered and made my way down the steps until I could peer into the first floor. Clutching the towel close to avoid exposing myself, I called again, "Who's there?"

"Ma'am, I'm so sorry. It's me, Evan. I'll leave now."

"Who the hell's Evan?" I craned my neck, twisting it nearly upside down to look below the ceiling line.

An incredibly handsome set of features stared back at me. Liquidy brown eyes, tanned cheeks, dark blond hair that he flopped over intense brows with a sexy, wide hand. "I'm one of the workers. I was here yesterday morning? Left my stuff here."

"Oh, God, a worker. Just a worker," I whispered, nearly collapsing on the stairs.

I froze there, pointlessly clutching terrycloth to my chest, because from where he stood, Evan could see right through me, into me, up me, and holy shit, the man was gorgeous. Grinning mischievously at me in my towel like a Cheshire cat.

"I'm sorry to scare you, ma'am."

Ma'am? He better stop with that ma'am business. Ma'am was what I called 70-year-old Betty back home. My guess was that Evan was in his mid-thirties, which left me feeling a little self-conscious but also not giving a shit in any way. So, I was older than him. Big, hairy deal. Did it matter? It wasn't like we were hooking up. I was here to do a job, not get with Evan.

Still, I had not gazed upon a man this beautiful since…well, since Jax at the airport, to be fair, but before that, it'd been years. We didn't get men like this in Melville—hunky men with chiseled faces, boy-like charm, and biceps to break down walls. We mostly got beer-can-toting men in football sweatshirts.

I tore my gaze away. "Nobody told me someone would be here this morning."

"That's my mistake, ma'am—"

"—Katja." I ventured another look at him.

"Katja." His stare could melt my panties. If I were wearing any. "Lily asked me to come by and get at least one A/C unit running for you before I start tearing down walls, but she never said you were here already. I thought you were arriving tonight."

"Welp, I've arrived. I'm here. Look at me, I've come."

I've come? Ugh.

My arms slapped my sides, making my towel start to slip. I secured it in place while cringing at how idiotic I sounded. I should've run back upstairs, leaving a Katja-shaped cloud in my place.

Evan held a perplexed smile, looked at the level in his hands, and shook his head, as if not knowing what to say. Good Lord, if we were in a movie, I'd forget making him state his purpose and demand he put that level down, come upstairs right this very moment, and prove himself worthy of breaking and entering. I knew that was my starved body talking, however, and not my common sense.

"I go get dressed now. That would be the proper thing to do," I muttered under my breath, turning to go.

Thankfully, someone else arrived to relieve me of making a fool of myself, and that was an old woman talking to Evan at the door. "Is she here?"

"Yep. Right up there." Evan pointed up the stairwell. Peeking down again, I could see the devilish upturn of his lips. "In her towel."

"Oh, you fresh one, you," the old woman said, pushing her way inside and staring up the stairwell. "Miss Miller? It's me, Nanette, your neighbor. Lily asked me to come check on you. Do you need anything?"

Only for the hot repair guy to use his tools on me, but other than that, not really. "I'm fine, thank you. Does everyone get such an early start around here?"

"I'm afraid so, yes. Would you like me to get coffee going for you while you get dressed?"

She didn't have to do that. Nobody had to do anything for me. I'd come here to work, yet everyone was being so nice, treating me like royalty. How could I say no? "That actually sounds lovely. Thank you."

"You're very welcome. Want me to get rid of Evan for you, too, so you can start your day in peace and quiet instead of dealing with his unique brand of troublemaking?"

"That's alright." I locked eyes with Evan's mischievous ones. "I like trouble."

6

Upstairs, I got dressed quickly, clumsily, thinking about what I would say to that man—that hot, hot fix-it man—when I came downstairs. I was pretty sure some type of flirting was going on between us, and flirting wasn't something I was used to anymore. It'd been more than twenty-two years since I'd flirted with anyone, and even then, it'd been a more subdued, innocent, small-town kind of flirting with whatever boys lingered after church.

Granted, Skeleton Key was a small town, too, but that man rummaging through his toolbox downstairs was a whole new level of hardbody I wasn't used to. In the bathroom, I checked my hair—ratty, pale brown, thin, too long, split ends. Perimenopause had already begun kicking in and I was suddenly feeling self-conscious about it.

"It's fine. You look fine." I headed down, the confidence I'd boldly displayed a few minutes before dissolving behind me as I clomped downstairs in my dollar store sneakers. When I reached the foyer, I got a better look at my visitors.

"Hello," I said with a composed nod.

"Good morning!" Nanette was fairly short with gray, spiky hair. She wore a one-piece white cotton jumper, and what she had on made no difference, because all I could see was Evan in loose-fitted jeans and a black polo that accentuated sun-kissed forearms. Lordy.

The man cast a few amused glances my way. "Ah, she's dressed."

"I would've been sooner, had I known anyone would be here this morning," I said, feeling myself blush.

All traces of flirting escaped Evan's new, serious tone. "I should've knocked first. So sorry I barged in. I honestly thought there was no one here." He dipped his head in apology.

"Thanks." I wrung my hands. "Guess I should get used to the fact that people will be coming and going throughout the day, right?"

Nanette poured coffee into a gray mug resembling a lump of clay with fins. "Actually, yes. Lily wants to have this place turned around in two months' time, which isn't very long, so this house will be very busy in the coming weeks. Vanilla creamer? Sugar?"

"Both, thanks. Is that a, uh..." I pointed at the mug.

She glanced at her hands. "A manatee, yes."

"Manatee." I snapped my fingers. "That's what I was going to say."

From the other room, I heard Evan snicker.

I wandered into the kitchen, taking in the full scope of the downstairs part of the house, as bright light filled every dusty corner. "Which house do you live in?" I asked Nanette.

She pointed through the front window at the second house on the right. "See the gray one next to the yellow one? That's me. Your next-door neighbor is a snowbird, Mr. Phelps. We rarely see him. I'll leave you my number in case you need anything. But text me first. I may be retired, but I belong to four social groups that meet every week, so if you just drop in, I probably won't be home."

"Got it, thanks." I tried the coffee but sweat had already broken out on my forehead and over my top lip. Sexy. Ice water was probably a better idea.

"What's your plan for today?" Nanette set her own finished manatee mug o' coffee in the dishwasher.

I sighed a little too loudly. "Getting started, I guess. Lots of boxes to sort through upstairs and several trunks, too. I'm looking forward to organizing everything."

"Really?" Evan poked his head around the corner.

"Yeah, actually. I've had an…interesting last several months, so this'll be the perfect distraction. As the old saying goes, 'A bad day organizing a beach house is better than a good day facing divorce.'"

Evan chuckled and disappeared again, but I could still hear him from the living room. "I don't think that's how the saying goes."

"It's something like that." I turned up a grin.

"Oh, that reminds me…" Nanette perked up. "I have the keys to the trunks to give you. Lily gave them to me this morning on her way out."

"Her way out?"

"Of town. She'll be in Atlanta for a day. When she returns, she'll be off to Austin after that. The woman's a whirlwind lately. She didn't want to wake you, so I've got them."

"Thanks, I'll take them, but uh, one of those trunks opened by itself this morning."

"Oh?" Nanette raised an eyebrow.

On the other side of the kitchen counter, Evan peered at me with those winsome eyes. "See?" he said to Nanette. "I'm not the only one hearing noises."

"You've heard it squeaking open, too?" I asked.

He nodded, wide-eyed. "Oh, yeah. But every time I go up there to check it out, I find nothing. There's not a whole lot left upstairs to creak. Granted, the windows are open, but what would make that kind of noise?"

"Iguanas. There was one in the room today, too. Freaked me out for a second. As for the trunk, it was wide open. Inside were all sorts of costumes, fabrics, teacups. Weird things to have in one box."

"Fabrics?" Nanette asked. "I'll have to take a look and see if there's anything I can use. I'm pretty sure Mrs. Fletcher would let me have them."

"Is that the lady who lived here before?" I asked.

"Yes, although they did say we could have whatever was left behind. I don't think they have any intention of coming back for their belongings." Nanette stared thoughtfully out the kitchen window.

"Do you sew?" I asked.

She whirled back to me. "I used to. Don't have time anymore, but I do love looking through scrap bins at the fabric stores. Do you?"

"I haven't made anything in a hot second, but I love rescuing fabrics and figuring out what to do with them. Maybe I'll make a throw cushion or two for my bed."

"Well, if you want to rummage through the boxes I have at home, you're welcome to," Nanette said. "Just text first."

"I will." If she collected fabrics, then she had to have… "Do you have a sewing machine?"

"I do, but the spooling mechanism gets stuck every time. You can use it if you can get it running correctly."

"I can take a look at it, Nanette," Evan offered.

"You've got enough on your plate, Evan."

"Honestly, I don't mind," he said.

"You know what? I probably won't have time to make anything anyway," I said, setting down the coffee. It was too hot in the house to drink. I searched the cabinets for an empty water glass.

Nanette jangled her keys. "I'll leave you to your work then. It was nice meeting you, Katja, and if you need a stun gun to keep this one in his place, it's right here." She patted a corner kitchen drawer and gave me a stern, I-got-you-girl look.

"Hey, I resemble that remark." Evan gave his power drill a turn, as he snapped a new nib into place. "Wait, there's not really a stun gun in there, is there?"

"You don't want to find out." Nanette shot him a cold glare before slipping out the door.

Leaving me alone. With Prince of the Power Tools. I swallowed and pretended to be checking my phone. "She's protective. I wonder what you've done to deserve that." I cut through the living room to the back window. Another gorgeous day in paradise. I glanced back at Evan.

"Nothing." He put away the drill nibs in the toolbox. "She just sees a guy my age and assumes I'm up to no good. I swear, I don't have any reputations preceding me."

"Mm, hmm. So, will you be here all day?" I asked, trying not to sound like I was too interested in his whereabouts. After all, I was here to work, not play, and I was also in the middle of an interminable divorce. Besides, I wasn't 100% sure Evan was interested in me that way.

"I'll be here as long as it takes to cool you down."

My stomach flipped. "Excuse me?" Never mind that last part. Maybe he really *was* into me.

"To get the A/C running?" He shook his head, smiling. "Upstairs, in your room? Beach breezes will only go so far in summer. Oh, man, foot-in-mouth disease is a terrible thing."

Nanette was right—Evan was dangerous, and after all I'd been through over the last seven months, I should probably steer clear, even though I was having fun flirting. As handsome as he was, he probably had women lined up around the block pining for a date. He didn't need a frumpy older woman to mess with, and I was no doubt nothing but a forgettable plaything.

"Alright, well…I'll be upstairs, working." I gave him a guarded smile then headed up, my knees wobblier than Jell-O after a 3 AM encounter with aliens. Firmly away from Evan's entrancing aura, I let go a huge sigh. "Geez." The iguana was no longer there. I stuck my head out the window to see where it might've gone, but apparently, the day had heated up enough to go back outside.

Time to get to work. I started with the open trunk, pulling items out and creating three piles—stuff Lily might want to keep, stuff to donate, and stuff Nanette or I might want to sort through. I figured Lily might want the porcelain or china tea sets for the bed-and-breakfast, the costumes were to donate, and the fabrics went into the Nanette and Katja pile. The more I looked at the costumes to give away, however, the more I wanted to keep those as well. Could cut them into scraps. On second thought, this was a difficult task for someone who'd lived without much her whole life. Every item looked like treasure!

After a while, I heard Evan's heavy footsteps coming upstairs and his voice announcing, "Coming through," as a warning.

"In here," I called from the floor, surrounded by the trunk items.

He paused at the bedroom door. "How's it going?"

"Slowly. I can see why she needed someone for two months."

"I would give you a hand, but I've got my own orders."

"It's okay. What else did she hire you to do besides fix the A/C and tear down a wall?" I opened a little red sequined purse to make sure there was nothing in it before tossing it into the discard pile.

"Combine the two downstairs rooms to make it more open and airy, then start working on the exterior while other guys redo the entire kitchen. Hey." He paused to lean on the door frame. "Sorry if I sounded like a jerk before. I always make the mistake of assuming other people are flirts like me. I must've gotten the sense you were."

"You're good. That was probably my own fault for staring at you. You're easy on the eyes, not gonna lie." I swiped my hair up and tied it into a knot.

"Wow, thanks." He looked genuinely surprised by my compliment.

"Come on. It's true. You must hear that a lot."

"Actually, I don't. I appreciate it."

We looked at each other another moment, then I got back to sorting. "Anyway, I'm just coming out of ending a marriage… I don't even know what to think or what I want half the time, so I'm sorry, too, if I seem out of sorts."

He nodded. "I get it. I just didn't want you to think I was an asshole or anything. I love meeting new people. We don't get too many around here, so it was nice to see a new face—a pretty one, at that."

My cheeks and neck flushed. I couldn't remember the last time anyone told me I was pretty. I didn't think Nathan had ever told me once. "Thanks. I can tell you that repairmen don't look like you do back where I live either. Usually, butt cracks are hanging out the back of their jeans."

Evan pretended to lower his pants. "I can pull mine down, if it makes you feel more at home."

I laughed a little too loudly and nervously. "Thanks, but no thanks," I said, even though the thought of him doing so set my body on fire. Why was this man wasting his time on me? Didn't he have some young island chick to charm the booty shorts off of?

"Alright, getting to the A/C unit in your room. Did you want to check things before I go in there?"

Check things? Did he think I had a box of sex toys sitting on the bed or something? "Nah, you're fine. Have at it."

"Wish me luck."

"Good luck! And do your best, please. I'm the one who has to sleep up here tonight."

He popped his head in again. "I will do my best." With a wink, he shuffled off, tools jangling from his belt like the chains of some forlorn, Victorian ghost.

For hours, I worked to sort, organize, and move boxes. I could've used Evan's help lowering a few, but I decided not to enlist his help. Seemed like he needed to stay focused on his work as much as I needed to stay focused on mine, but the truth was, I couldn't stop thinking about him in here, stripping wire, wrenching away old bolts, and lying on the floor three paces from where I slept.

By lunchtime, I'd gotten through half the boxes in the guest room and emptied out the first trunk as well. In the fridge was a pitcher of something that looked like lemonade, and I knew, just by looking at it, that I would down the whole thing in one fell swoop. That's how hot it was in the house.

When I poured myself a glass, my stomach exploded into glittery fireworks. Key lime lemonade, it had to be. I was about to ask Evan if he'd like some, when from upstairs, I heard a joyous whoop. "It's running!"

"It's running?" I called back.

"Come feel it!" Evan yelled.

By the time I reached him upstairs, he was doing a little dance in front of the A/C, twerking his butt in front of the vents. "A triumph!" I laughed.

"Hell, yeah. Come on…aw, yeah…it's working…it's working…I did it…it's cold…come feel it." He reached for my hand and yanked me toward him, and oh yes, that was some nice, frigid air blowing out the unit.

"Because of you, I will un-melt. I will coalesce into solid form once again. I appreciate it so much," I said, infusing as much sincerity as I could into my words, adding a tiny applause.

Evan slid his tools into his belt, ran a hand through his dark blond hair, and bowed. "I may not be good at everything, but what I'm good at, I'm very good."

"Oh…" I was at a loss for words.

"In other words, at your service, ma'am." He bowed.

"Hey, about that ma'am stuff? It's just Katja."

"Well, Katja, if there's any other way I can be of service…" He looked up at me with those dark eyes underneath soft, sexy brows. Whatever these words were coming out of his mouth, he meant them. "Just let me know."

Lordy, lord, lord, lord.

I gulped and moved past him to stand in front of the A/C vent, letting cold air douse me completely. Evan, if he stuck around long enough, would be the death of me. But it would be a good death. A sexy death. A long overdue orgasmic death.

"Nanette was right about you. Now shoo. Go, before you get me in trouble."

"I thought you loved trouble." He gave me a roguish smile before backing out the door and was off downstairs. "See you in a few days."

"Goodbye, Evan."

The moment he left, I threw myself onto the bed. What was this life? I felt like I'd left the harsh reality of Melville and entered an Aaron Spelling sit-com. What the heck was I going to do with that man? My body could think of at least a million things, but all of them would be unprofessional. Would Ms. Lily think she'd hired the wrong person if she found me flirting with her fix-it guy? Would it look wrong to the world if I flirted while still technically married? Did it even matter?

Of course, all this was assuming he was even seriously interested in me, that he wasn't just yanking a bored housewife's chain, that I had the balls to invite him into my bed, that I could get past who I was and move toward who I wanted to be. But I knew the chances were low, because even now, laying here, staring at the ceiling fan, all I could hear in my head was Nathan's derisive voice.

You think anybody's going to look at you?

You honestly think a younger guy really wants what you have to offer?

Who would want to get with an old mom, Katja? One with that spare tire around her belly and saggy arms. Give me a break—that dude is just bored. Only man who might love you looking the way you do is me. And even I left.

7

The days blended together like rum, sugar, and lime.

My hope, considering how many times I had to stand up and sit down repeatedly, was to minimize strenuous effort. Even though there was A/C in my room now, the rest of the house was still hot. Which was why I decided on tackling one bedroom at a time rather than moving all over the place.

By the end of the fifth day, I'd sorted through one bedroom's worth of junk. So far, I'd set aside for Lily: two tea sets, a small gramophone, a collection of vintage classical record albums, a crystal ball that might look good with her collection and *Dead & Breakfast* theme, a silver candelabra (why the previous owners didn't want this was amazing to me), and several real-deal, embossed silver-plated trays that would've given *HomeGoods* a run for their money.

Evan had only come back once, two days ago, to measure the living room walls and mark Xs on stuff to be torn down. He'd come in talking on his cell, lifted his chin to me in greeting, then left, still talking on his cell. I had to admit I was disappointed he hadn't stayed longer.

Not that I needed to hop into another man's arms or anything, but I'd been cooped up for three days straight, and it would've been nice to talk to another live human being.

Nanette had brought me three meals for three days in a row, and yesterday's had been some sort of fried seafood, though I wasn't exactly sure—some sort of round, delicious balls of fishy thang. Whatever it was, it was magical. I'd been upstairs at the time, so Nanette had yelled, "Leaving you food!" up into the echoey, square stairwell. When I'd stuck my head over the railing to thank her, I saw she had a young person with her— skinny, boyish, hands stuck in pockets, streaks of purple in their otherwise short brown hair.

I'd waved at whoever he, she, they were.

By late afternoon, I'd moved my cleaning efforts into the next room where I tried to use the key Nanette had given me to open the second trunk, but the key wouldn't work. It was one of those old-style metal keys that you had to twist just right to get the lock to open, and this one seemed like it'd been twisted too hard. I couldn't line it up correctly and thought it could benefit from a good straightening. Taking it downstairs, I reached into Evan's toolkit, the one he left here every day, to search for a hammer. Inside I found a folded stack of paper.

Now, my grandmother had raised me to respect other people's belongings. Heck, I wasn't even allowed to look through her purse until the day she went into the hospital complaining of chest pain. But this was Evan's toolkit, and Evan hadn't been here in two days, and I was feeling in need of a bit of human connection. For all I knew, the papers were just an invoice or stack of receipts, but regardless, I wanted an inkling, anything, into his life. I unfolded them.

Sketches. Beautiful architectural designs of gorgeous homes surrounded by palm trees, presumably in the Keys, all marked with labels and arrows and measurements in some of the neatest handwriting I'd ever seen. Design #2, Design #6, Design #11, each one more gorgeous than the next. What was he doing fixing A/C units in old houses when he should've been building dream homes for dream clients?

It wasn't my business, that's what.

I folded the pages, found the hammer, and pounded the key flat on top of the toolkit. Looked straight enough to me. I put everything back where I found it, closed the toolkit, and headed back to the stairs where I froze in my tracks. There, midway up the steps, was a shimmering blue ball of light, a pulsating swirl of buzzing energy, hovering two feet above the steps. I sucked in a gasp.

What the heck?

I stared, as it swirled and pulsed and breathed and—I know how this will sound—looked at me.

Lily's words echoed in my mind—*this island has its…idiosyncrasies.* Yeah, well, one of her idiosyncrasies was staring me in the face, and I had no knowledge on what it was or how to get rid of it.

"What?" I asked the ball of light. "What…what do you want?" It occurred to me that I was tired after texting the girls for hours last night, letting them know what was going on with their father, the way he was demanding to know where I was for days, and how they were, under no circumstances whatsoever, to inform him of my whereabouts.

I dropped to my knees, unable to hold myself up anymore. Despite the cold air blasting in my room, I hadn't slept. And now I was staring at a blue ball of electricity. A ball I was fairly certain had a brain, an intelligence of its own. As I watched from the floor, mesmerized, the ball began to float upwards, into the stairwell, rather than up the stairs. With shaking hands, I got to my feet and slowly headed up, gripping the handrail with sweaty hands.

The thing rose toward the second floor then hovered over the landing before I could reach it. For a moment, it disappeared out of my line of sight, as I realized how incredibly cold it had suddenly grown in the stairwell and hugged my sweaty, dirty tank top to fight off the chill. When I reached the second floor, I watched the light move into the room where I'd been working and hurried to catch up to it, but the moment I ducked inside, the light had dissipated.

I searched the hall, the stairs, and every room on the second level. No ball of light, but my heart was pounding like a runaway train pummeling through a station at a hundred miles per hour. What was that thing? Was there some sort of electric light phenomena in the Keys that I didn't know about? Some sort of tropical version of aurora borealis that appeared indoors in the middle of the day to unsuspecting women while alone in their place of employment? It could happen.

My eyes flew open.

The trunk was open.

The trunk that, a minute ago, had been tightly locked. The one I'd gone downstairs to hammer out the key for—the one that wouldn't budge when I'd yanked. Now it yawned wide open. Out of the corner of my eye, something green flashed, and I caught its reflection in the sun—the iguana. He was basking in the heat of the late afternoon with the sun's rays directly hitting him on the windowsill, all stretched out from nose to tail like a serene green relic of prehistoric times.

I clutched my chest. "Don't, don't do that. Don't scare me like that."

Iggy twitched his tail.

"Did you see it?" I asked. "Did you see the…the…goddammit…the light? That was in here just now?" I pointed my shaking finger. My god, I couldn't think of common, everyday words.

Iggy rolled his googly eyes at me. Something about his chill attitude told me I should just chill myself. Whatever it was, it hadn't been dangerous. Maybe curious to know what I was doing or who I was, but not dangerous. After all, I was the stranger here, going through trunks of people's belongings. Who was I to handle other people's things? Who was I to hold the teacups of those who'd drunk from them during another era? I was sure that had to disturb the continuity fabric of time and space somehow.

Iggy seemed to say, *Well, the trunk you wanted open so badly is now open, so who cares about your stupid ball of light?*

He was right.

Sliding the key into my shorts' pocket, I looked into the open trunk with equal parts fascination and fear.

Inside were bolts of fabrics—red velvets, blue satins, black lace trim, white lace trim. I pulled them out, one by one, propping them against the wall, turning back to the trunk and falling deeper into its musty-smelling depths until I reached underneath and pulled out an arm.

"Gah!" I screamed, throwing the arm on the floor, kicking it into the hallway. A plastic part from a baby doll rolled and skittered along the wood planks, disappearing through the spindles of the stairwell railing and falling to its death. "What the?"

Lord, I needed to chill the heck out or I'd die of fright. "Let's try that again." I reached into the trunk, pulled out a tangle of feathers and more sheets of velvet until I saw them—plastic arms, but also legs, shiny loops of hair, and plastic eyeballs in gemstone colors staring and winking at me.

Dolls. Six or seven of them, all ten to twelve inches tall, the baby kind, not the Barbie kind, sat underneath the piles of fabric on the bottom of the trunk. Two were white "skin" with blond curls and red plaited hair, but four had varying shades of tan to brown "skin" with long brown or black braided hair, and pretty pink smiles.

I lifted one up to examine her. She was scuffed, scratched, possibly even bitten. In desperate need of polishing up and starting over, but there was something sweet about her. As I stared into her glassy brown eyes, I suddenly felt I knew love. And imagination. And loneliness. Some little girl had played with these long ago.

"Who would leave these, Iggy?" I set the doll on the floor, bending her legs, so she could "sit." Carefully, I lifted the other ones, too, and placed them in a row beside her sisters.

Once the trunk was empty, I counted twelve bolts of fabric, nine spools of trim, six more feather boas, a cowboy hat, eighteen (yes, eighteen) pairs of brown, black, or white nylon stockings, seven dolls, and the crazy-ass notion that I needed to entertain them after they'd been stuck inside a box for so long.

"Be right back," I told no one.

Darting into the other bedroom, I retrieved two pink teacups and returned, taking a seat in front of the dolls. I proceeded to set up the cups in front of the dolls' feet, artfully arranging everybody so it looked like they were having a tea party.

"There you go. Wait, one more thing…" I reached for a feather boa then wound it around the line of dolls, so each of them got to wear a small section of it. "Now, you can have fun."

I smiled. Clearly, I was the one having fun. Here I thought I'd spend the day searching through more old clothes and other people's discarded things when I'd stumbled onto these little treasures, as dirty and worn as they were, and there was a tea set, and costumes, and dolls, and a ghost light, and an iguana named Iggy, who was not on the windowsill anymore.

Wait, what? I stood and stuck my head out the window. Gone. Where did he go so fast?

I heard my phone vibrate along the old pine floor. It didn't ring very often, but each time it did, it practically sent me packing. As I feared, it was Nathan.

"No." I crossed my arms defensively over my chest.

Don't answer that, Katja, Nana said.

"I wasn't going to."

I wouldn't know what to say anyway. He was calling to find out where I was. And even though common sense and the laws of scorned women everywhere told me he had no right to know, I didn't feel that way inside. I felt like he still owned me, a feeling I had to obliterate, one way or another.

Although, what if it was important? What if he was ready to sign the divorce settlement agreement and just had a question? What if it was about one of the girls? What if, what if, what if?

It's not, Nana said. *He just wants to control you. You need to stop caring.*

Damn it, Nana, I know that! If I could've stopped caring what he thought of me, I would've done it a long time ago. I clutched my ponytail while waiting for the phone to stop ringing and alert me to voicemail. Because I knew he'd leave a message this time. I felt it coming. Sure enough, I got the voicemail alert and tapped it so I could listen.

"Where the hell are you? I came home so we could talk, it's been a week, and you're still not here. Where'd you go, Katja? Huh? Who the fuck paid for you to leave town? Because I know your job at *Bill's Pharmacy* couldn't have gotten you very far. Fine, I didn't want to tell you this on the phone, but I wanted to come home. I wanted to see you again. I made a mistake. I know that. Call me back."

Click.

He'd gone asking people in town. Someone told him where I'd worked. Good thing I hadn't told anyone I was headed to Florida.

"No." I shook my head. No way, José, was he coming back into my life. I may have had a hard time getting his influence out of my head, but I knew a liar when I heard one. Two, maybe three months ago, I might've taken him back. He was my husband, after all, and we could work this out, but now I was in Skeleton Key, working for celeb chef, Lily Autumn, living in a haunted house less scary than Nathan Miller, and there was no way.

No *fucking* way.

I stormed out of the house, leaving my phone behind again, so I wouldn't be tempted to answer texts I could hear now coming in. I'd been working eight straight hours anyway. I plowed through the hot sand and dunked myself, for the first time ever, fully clothed, into the ocean. Warm, salty water embraced me, filled my mouth when I sobbed, and told me it was going to be okay. He couldn't hurt me, the ocean said. I wished I could believe her. Look what he'd done to my confidence.

Should I leave?

Was this a sign it was time to go home?

Because unlike the strange goings-on of the Berry House, Nathan was a real, live person who could get into our car and drive a thousand miles to find me and take me back to Melville with him if he wanted to. What Nathan wanted, Nathan got, so as long as he didn't know where I was, all would be fine.

All will be fine, I repeated for the next hour, letting the soft waves rock and swish me around until the sun dropped below the horizon, until tangerine clouds turned to royal purple skies, and down the beach near Lily's house, a bonfire sprouted. Around it were women, dancing, laughing, and celebrating, and I knew, in an instant, who they were.

8

Lily's neighbors, Heloise and Jeanine, were one of the best things about the show, *Witch of Key Lime Lane*. For months, I loved tuning in to watch their quiet cosmic energy, the kind of camaraderie that turned glasses of wine into unapologetic singing, dancing, and laughter on the back porch. Bonus that they also cooked and baked for guests, as well as gave meditation classes.

I walked toward them along the cool sand under the moonless sky, stopping beside a palm tree to check out a glass ball wound around the trunk and tucked underneath a coil of rope.

The ladies spotted me and called out, "Hello!"

"Katja!" Lily waved her arms.

I felt sheepish interrupting whatever they had going on, but they gave off such a high, positive energy, that my depleted soul naturally drifted over to them. "Hi," I said shyly.

Lily tripped over her own foot, cackled, and laced an arm around my shoulder. "Guys, here she is. Meet Katja!"

"Hey, Katja!" Heloise said, warm brown eyes and skin shining in the firelight. Something about her instant

71

hug without condition nearly made me break into tears. She was like the sisterly aunt I didn't know I needed.

Jeanine refilled her glass of wine and extended it out to me. "Here, have mine. We only brought out three glasses."

"Oh, no, thank you. It's okay. I'm interrupting."

"Really, it's okay. You sure?"

"Yeah, I'm good. Thank you. I was just swimming in the ocean when I saw you all come out here. You were having so much fun, I had to see what you were up to."

"This is the part they don't show on TV, girl," Heloise laughed, lifting the cutting board covered in charcuterie. "If they did, we'd have a very concerned viewership. Prosciutto?"

"Oo, thanks." That, I would take. I was starving after a day of sweating and sorting and had just run out into Mother Ocean's arms after Nathan's text assault.

Lily plucked a cracker off the board and slapped some cheese on it. "Heloise is kidding. We don't do anything terrible out here."

"But I'm not, though," Heloise added. "If people really saw what we did around here…"

I always did wonder if their witchy friendship was genuine in real life. So far, this raucous bonfire seemed like strong evidence to me.

"Actually, Katja," Lily said, "I'm glad I found you out here. I feel horrible that we haven't welcomed you officially yet."

"I know. What's up with that, Pulitzer?" Jeanine lifted her arms to the sky and stretched. "I thought by now you'd have rolled out the red carpet, made a seven-tiered cake in the shape of a dildo…something."

Heloise burst out laughing so hard, she nearly fell over. It was clear they'd had a little too much wine, which did put a much-needed smile on my face. Jeanine, out of breath from her own joke, caught her wife, while Lily tucked her tongue into her cheek.

"You know damn well I don't need one, Jeanini Panini. Not when I've got it live in the flesh." She rose her eyebrows in secret communication, and the two older ladies looked at each other.

"What's the harm in having a backup?" Jeanine asked then looked at me. "Am I right?"

I shrugged. "I wouldn't know. I haven't slept with anyone or any*thing* in over seven months."

"Is that right?" Heloise cocked her head, genuinely concerned.

I nodded.

She gave me a sad smile. "I see nothing wrong with that. Sometimes we need time to ourselves."

Lily showed me to a beautifully set table with gold tablecloth, split coconut shells holding candles, and crystals scattered about. "Guys, you just met Katja one minute ago, and this is the conversation you loop her into?" She shook her head. "I swear, I can't with you two."

"It's okay," I whispered. "I think they're awesome."

"That, they are. Okay, listen, this has been a super busy week with Atlanta, then Austin, and I didn't want to overwhelm you with too much, but *nowww* that you've had a chance to settle down… Katja, would you like to come over tomorrow night? Around 8 PM?"

"Oh. I, uh…"

"You can meet some of the other neighbors and staff. They can all meet you. An official welcome!" Her amber eyes reflected the crackling embers.

"Wow, sure!" I said, tossing up my arms. "I honestly didn't expect an official welcome of any kind. I'm just so thrilled to be here with you all." I looked at everyone's faces staring back at me all melty like I'd said something sweet.

"Well, we're happy you're here," Heloise said. "We know the tough time you've had."

"Yeah," I sighed, swiping a butter cracker and piece of salami off the tray. "It's not weird that everyone knows about my life—it's the same way in the town I'm from—but here, everyone is so frank and open about it. Y'all are like concerned family I didn't know I had."

"In other words, y'all are being nosy bitches," Jeanine told the other ladies.

"More like sisters I've never had." I laughed, although Sid was like an old uncle.

"You'll get used to us being in each other's business quite a bit," Heloise said. "So, what's got you out here night swimming? Ex giving you trouble?"

I supposed it was easy to guess. Jeanine polished off her wine and fished around the board for a good piece of cheese.

"You are not required to answer any of our nosy questions, Katja," Lily said.

But I did want to answer. I'd needed to talk about it for a while now. In Melville, I'd been the

GABRIELLE KEYES

outsider. Never mind that I'd lived there twenty-two years, I was still seen as the girl from out of town, the girl Nathan married and brought to live there, yet I'd never been fully accepted by the community. I didn't have many friends, and the ones I did have were all sweet, churchgoing older ladies who would never talk about divorce or dildos.

"He thinks he owns me," I blurted, staring into the fire.

Three sets of groans echoed around me. "What is it with these men?" Lily asked Heloise and Jeanine. "They ruin your life, then when you try to make a life of your own, they have to go and ruin that, too."

"Yes!" I whipped her way. "Why do they do that?"

"They don't all do that, by the way," Heloise interjected. "Some were raised right and genuinely want to see you happy."

"Fine, maybe your ex," Lily said. "But then there's the Dereks and the…" She looked at me.

"Nathans."

"The Nathans," she said. "Who can't stand to see you happy. To see you succeeding without them."

"Who hate the fact that you've moved on without their help, even though they're the ones who made you move on in the first place," I said.

"Exactly." Lily shot out a fist and I bumped it. "I know you just got here, and we have no business offering unsolicited advice, but can I just say one thing?"

"Of course. I mean, *pfft*, my goodness, it's not every day I've got Lily Autumn giving me relationship advice."

"Oh, well, I don't know that I'm the best to give anyone life advice, but…don't feed into it."

I squinted. "Into…"

"Into his bullshit. Try as he might to get you to give up your energy, don't give it to him. Your safe space that you've created for yourself? That's sacred. Guard it. It's what will eventually set you free." Her emphatic pointing told me she was still angry about her own experience. As she should be, and to think hers had been public!

"I'm not free. I'm tethered. To everything he says, to his texts, to his opinion of me. It's because I allowed it for so long. So, now, I'll feel guilty if I don't answer when he calls. You don't understand, Nathan was more than just my husband. He was…" Ugh, I hated to say it, but it was true. "He was my keeper."

"Oh, no." Heloise shook her head.

"That's not good," Jeanine added.

Lily watched me carefully, her eyes boring intention and protection into my skull. "We need to change that, Katja. He doesn't own you, and you don't owe him anything else. You already gave him children and years of your life. He chose another route. Enough is enough. From now on, it's your life."

I knew she was right. I needed to hear it from someone who'd lived through it, too. I knew what I had to do was march back to that haunted, old house with the weird balls of light and creepy old dolls, neither of which were scarier than Nathan, and block his number on my phone.

"And what more perfect night to do it than tonight." When Heloise smiled, she carried grace and wisdom in her eyes. "It's a New Moon." She gave me her own wine glass and took Jeanine's to share. Lily lifted her glass, I lifted Heloise's, and the three met in the middle.

"I want you to say this…" Lily held my gaze for a moment, as tears sprouted on my lower lids. How many nights had I cried now? Too many. "Say, 'Tonight, I let you go, Nathan.' Go on…"

"Tonight, I let you go, Nathan," I said, doing my best to feel the words.

"From this point on, you won't control me."

"From this point on, you won't control me." Tears slipped down my salt-stained cheeks.

"From this point on, I make my own choices, my own decisions…" Lily said it with conviction I couldn't feel, and that upset me. I wanted—needed—to feel it. I wanted to be free.

I swiped at my eyes and let out a breath. "From this point on, I make my own choices, my own decisions," I repeated, then added my own words. "Also, Nathan, you will not demand to know where I am. You will leave me alone, to live in peace and tranquility."

Lily gave a slow nod. "Yes, you've got it."

"She's good," Jeanine said to Heloise.

"So mote it be." Fire flickered in Lily's eyes.

I wasn't sure what that meant, but if it was coming from these ladies, it had to be alright. "So mote it be."

"Blessed be!" the three said together.

In their eyes and faces, I knew I'd made the right decision to come to Skeleton Key. If earlier I'd doubted whether I should've left home in the first place, if I'd felt guilty for running off unannounced, these ladies made it all worthwhile. Money wasn't the only thing I'd needed when I arrived nearly a week ago. People—I'd needed good, kindhearted people.

Yes, Katja, Nana's voice slipped through my mind. *Very good. And now, go back and block the motherfucker.*

9

I woke up in a fiery heat, like my body combusting from the inside out. When I sat up gasping for air, I couldn't believe the amount of sweat beading, dripping off my skin. My T-shirt clung to me like a wet rag. What on Earth?

I checked the time—2:29 AM. Another message from Nathan sat on my phone, but I wouldn't read it. No way, no how. Not while I was alone in a house that wasn't mine, in a body that didn't feel like mine either. I had no witchy support system around me now and enough to deal with without him.

Nana wanted me to block him, and I would. I just needed courage, and knowing me, it would come in my own time, like it did when applying for this job. I needed to be ready, and I wasn't.

I slithered out of bed, stood in front of the A/C with my arms out in the hopes of cooling the hot flashes. I used to sleep well, but not anymore. Everything seemed to be changing—my life, my body, my mind. Sometimes I wasn't even sure who I was, like a snake shedding its skin, or a caterpillar changing inside its awkward-looking cocoon.

Trudging to the bathroom, I tried to pee quick, because the more time I spent awake, the more I remembered that weird things had happened during the day that might not be as easy to swallow at night. If I heard trunks opening now, or saw dolls in the hallway, I might just vacate the premises without collecting a paycheck. I didn't feel the spiritual presence of the house was dark or menacing in any way. If anything, it was like a curious child.

I slipped out of the bathroom and climbed back into bed (on top of the sheets this time), when I became aware of a distant sound blending in with the ticking and cranking of the air conditioner motor, like one white noise above the other, which made it hard to notice at first, especially since I was half asleep.

But it sounded like cheering.

People applauding.

My brain searched for an explanation. Was it Saturday? Maybe some bar down the street was still hopping late into the night. There was music, too, but instead of a live band or modern dance tunes, or anything you might hear in the islands, this music sounded vintage and metallic, and played a little too fast, as if through an old victrola.

I sat on the edge of the bed listening, my eyes wide open in the dark. The music grew louder, closer, until it sounded like it was right outside on the beach. Maybe a party boat was passing in the night, though it would've been a 20s-themed party. When the A/C shut off, I thought maybe it was done with its cycle, but then I noticed the green ON light fading away, at the same time I heard the charging sound on my phone blink.

The power went out?

Great. For a second, the electricity came back, the phone dinged, and the A/C unit roared again, then it all turned off again. What in hellblazes was going on?

I could hear the music clearly again, definitely a 1920s song that a crowd was singing to. Men's voices. I stood and moved to the window, but it was coming more from my right, from the doorway into the hall. I didn't care for the darkness in the house, especially the pitch-black hallway, so I grabbed my phone and turned on the flashlight. Feeble light illuminated enough for me to set foot into the hall, where the music grew louder.

At the intersection of the two, opposing bedrooms, I wasn't sure which way the music was coming from, if it was even in the house at all. I still hadn't ruled out the most probable explanation, that someone was having a party on the beach, and the theme was Roaring 20's or Dapper Days. Beach weddings were popular, but wouldn't a beach wedding have started around the time I was swimming in the ocean?

Slowly, I stepped into the southernmost room and moved to the open window to glance down the length of the beach. Dizziness came over me, and I had to blink several times to adjust my vision in the darkness. I was exhausted from work, lightheaded from the hot flash, stressed from Nathan's texts, and now electrically charged. Though I stood on solid ground, I almost felt like I was buzzing—levitating—off the floor. My body was humming, feet grazing the wooden planks, and I suddenly knew—knew in my bones—that the music wasn't coming from the beach or the house.

It was coming from the closet.

Slowly, I turned and stared at the white, double-shuttered doors, reaching out to pull on the knobs with both hands, terrified of what I might find. With overwhelming relief, all I saw were wire hangers, boxes, and a pile of discarded shoes coalesced to look like a person slumped in the closet. Once I got past my initial gasp, I craned my neck into the space to gauge where the music was coming from. Maybe a speaker was still connected inside the walls or something.

The singing turned to more like alcohol-fueled chanting, then cheering, then loud applause made it easy for me to tell that it was coming from the left-hand side, which was impossible, because the left side of the closet was the outer wall of the house. There would be no door there. And yet, a small, dumbwaiter aperture appeared in the dark, one that remained closed until I stepped up to it and hoisted it open.

The house's wall space breathed hot and musty air into my face. The buzzing sensation below my feet intensified, the cheering grew, the music grew louder, and my lightheadedness expanded to include my entire body. I stepped into the wall space, feeling like I was supposed to. It was calling me. As the bowels of the house drew me in deeper, it occurred to me I might be dreaming. Yes, this was a lucid dream—it had to be. What else could explain how the steamy interior of the walls dissolved into a dark balcony overlooking a small, brightly-lit theater? Its auditorium was packed with men wearing rag-tag vintage clothing, not tuxedos or suits, but trousers and workmen's shirts, flat caps and suspenders, things men didn't wear today.

And there was a smell.

I covered my nose and mouth. The walls trapped stanky, sweaty, unholy body odor of thirty to forty men who'd obviously never heard of deodorant in their lives. Some sat politely in their seats, while some stood, and some even climbed onto the armrests, waving money, handkerchiefs, and hats at a woman on stage. A stunningly beautiful woman with medium-dark tawny skin and dark eyes, arched, discerning eyebrows, and rouged cheeks. Her mouth, delicately formed, was painted red, and she wore a red corset with black stockings, a red-and-black garter, and black feathers in her French-twisted hair. Despite being half naked, she was elegant, like a rare-breed flamingo with long, shiny legs. The men catcalled and wolf-whistled at her, but she didn't seem to mind. She relished in it, turning and posing, smiling for them, then turning again to look demurely over her shoulder.

"It's a dream," I murmured. "Gotta be."

I lingered in the shadows of the balcony while down the row, half the men cheered and fist-pumped. "Josephine! Take it off, Josephine!"

I looked at Josephine to see what she thought of the demands being made of her, and my first reaction was to tell her, *No, girl, don't do it. Have some self-respect.* But Josephine only turned, arched her back, and reached behind her slowly with one hand to undo one clasp at a time, taking her time about it, glancing back at the men with that artful raised eyebrow to egg them on. Josephine was a masterful actress who made these men believe she loved her job. They threw coins at her. They threw roses. Someone threw his glove. The cheering reached a fever pitch, as the men anticipated Josephine's final pose, then finally, with measured coyness, she pulled off the corset, leaving just her undies and stockings, exposing her bare back.

"Turn around, Josephine!" the man nearest to me kept yelling. He looked like he might fall over the balcony railing from how hard he was drooling. I thought of giving him a little shove to watch him fall over.

That seemed funny to me, so I giggled and suddenly, four pairs of eyes flipped my way. "Oh, uh…" I hadn't realized anyone could see me. Stepping backwards, so I could go back the way I'd come, I got tangled with a curtain. "Shit."

"Hey!" the man called, foggy alcohol-riddled gaze rippling across my face. "What are you doing there, little miss?"

"Me? I, uh…" His guess was as good as mine. I'd been in the closet one moment, and the next, here in this strange place, in another time, with men acting like dogs and a woman taking advantage from it. "What year is it?" I asked.

"Year?" The man's face twisted into a grimace. Yikes, someone did not like my question.

"You know what? Doesn't matter." I smiled and turned to leave. "I'll just go now."

"It's 1928," he replied. "Why are you hiding back there?"

"Who is she?" I pointed to the lady onstage, who had, by now, noticed me and was doing her best not to be distracted. Instead of showing her annoyance at the woman causing a fuss on the balcony, the one wearing a

T-shirt and bare legs, she gave me a worried, protective expression.

"Why, that's Josephine Berry. Anybody from around here knows that," the man scoffed and elbowed his taller buddy, who reacted as though his friend had delivered a hilarious retort to my perfectly legitimate question.

"I'm not from around here," I replied.

Go, Josephine mouthed at me from the stage, but I couldn't be sure she was addressing me or someone else. *Go...*

Yes, I should go. I'd intruded on her performance, and if she didn't deliver the goods, she'd miss out on her profits. These men were making their final purchases of the night, and she needed to pay her bills. Even though she didn't say so, I knew in my heart that she needed that money flying through the air. In this fevered dream, I glanced down at my feet, to make sure I wouldn't trip on anything else, and when I did, I noticed my feet were darker, smaller than my own.

I gasped, backed up, and slipped into the shadows, as the two men watched me, laughed, and shook their heads like I was the dumbest thing in the world, but was I me? Or was I in someone else's place? Because I felt confusion at watching Josephine dance, felt the displaced sense that I wasn't supposed to be in the balcony, and desperately wanted to go back to my room—not the room I was staying in, but the room belonging to the closet.

As I backed into the recesses, the theater was enshrouded in darkness again, the cheering faded, and I was alone in the bedroom, in the dizzying, electrifying heat that had transformed me. When I stumbled out of the closet, wondering what the heck had just happened, I tripped over something on the floor, something soft and gummy, and I had to hold onto the wall to keep from squishing it. Watching me from the floor, with his curious, large eyes, was Iggy, the iguana.

"You," I blurted. "What are you…" The question fell flat. What did it matter what the iguana was doing there? At least it belonged in this world. It was the theater and the quick jaunt back in time that was questionable.

I shuffled from the room, darting into my bedroom where I closed the door and sat cross-legged on the bed, rocking and telling myself that everything was fine. My heart raced a thousand miles a minute. I reached for my phone to check the time and saw a barrage of texts coming in fast and furious.

HELLOOOOOOO

Are you really ignoring me?

Don't make me come and find you Kat

I couldn't deal with this. Not now. Not with all these strange things happening to me in the same day. With shaking fingers, I managed to press the "i" next to his name, located the choices of action for the selected phone number, and hit BLOCK.

10

My room was cold—my bed, toasty.

Without opening my eyes, I remembered my dream last night—the one about walking into a closet and emerging out into a theater from the 1920s. After I'd managed to get back to my bedroom and fall asleep again, the dream had continued.

In it, Josephine herself had walked into my room wearing her red corset and black lace stockings. She'd stood at the edge of my bed, looking at me curiously. It was okay, she told me. It was okay for her to dance for men, to shake her body and take off her clothes if it made money and paid the bills and helped her take care of things. There was no shame in it, and I shouldn't feel sorry for her. We all did what we needed to do, she told me.

I wasn't sure why she felt the need to tell me all this. I was all for women making their own choices and had never, as far as I could remember, shamed anyone for it, but dreams were weird that way. Besides, she'd said, setting down a bouquet of roses on my comforter and opening a box of chocolates with a wave of her polished nails, most of them respected her. Adored her, even. If anything, they respected her *more* than other dancers and actresses, ballet dancers and opera performers, *because* she dared to go there, for their entertainment when no one else would. That's why they took such long train rides to see her. It was her beauty, her skin with its warm, honey tones, her demure eyes, her movements on the stage, and most of all, the toeing of the line between innocent and risqué that lured them in droves.

Point blank—she was good at what she did.

I understood all she was saying, but it still made me sad that she had to do it. That she couldn't just sell bottles of rum like Annie Jackson had to get by, that she had to perform on a nightly basis. Theater work was grueling. She didn't have to, she told me. She could work in the island resorts cleaning rooms, but she'd chosen to dance burlesque instead. It allowed her to work from home, to take care of her child at the same time.

I respect that, I'd told her. *Not judging you whatsoever.*

She'd smiled warmly with that perfect, wrinkle-free face, until I realized she'd said "take care of my child," because until that point in the dream, I hadn't realized she'd had a child. That would definitely be another reason why some people might judge her. Picking up another chocolate bon-bon, she'd bitten into it, shrugged, then twiddled her fingers goodbye. And then, she'd floated right out of my room as though she'd had no feet.

It had felt so real.

When I opened my eyes, I nearly scrambled for a piece of paper to jot it all down, settling for creating a note on my phone instead. It felt freakin' great not having any messages from Nathan. Then, I remembered—I'd blocked him. Last night. I was scared over what else he might do if I didn't. Knowing the way Nathan got whenever anybody defied him, I worried he'd seek out the girls, make them tell him where I was, but I was prepared to do whatever it took to protect them.

I did, however, have a text from Hailey:

Hi mom.

> *Hey, sweet girl.*
> *What is of the up?*

Not much. Finishing up my summer internship. Wanted to ask if you could help us with something.

> *What is it?*

Elly and Marlene, two of her friends, were planning on a weekend trip to South Carolina, and Hailey wanted to know if I could give her some travel money so she and Remy could go, too.

I let out a breath. First, I was glad the text wasn't about their father. Relieved it was about something normal. Second, I didn't have any money. Not yet, anyway, and I wouldn't feel comfortable asking Lily for an advance on my paycheck considering I'd only been working for a week.

> *When do you need it?*

I can pay for it now but

can you cover the cost later?

> *Sure, baby.*
> *I'll send some*
> *money soon.*

Yayyy, thank you mama!

> *Worth it.*

I'd wanted to eventually start saving—all my marriage, we'd lived paycheck to paycheck—but I also really wanted my girls to have a wonderful college experience, to make friends, and to live life to the fullest, even if it meant me having to work a bit harder. I was a mother, after all, and I lived vicariously through my kids. Besides, Hailey didn't ask for extras very often, and it gave me pleasure to know I was helping her out.

In the bathroom, I brushed my teeth, about to get dressed when I turned and saw him. Freaking Iggy, outside the bathroom door, sitting astride my sneakers like he wanted to get inside of them. The scream that shot out of my lips shook the entire house. Iggy had not, until now, scared me to that level, but I was already tense after weird dreams.

Someone knocked on the front door. "You," I snapped at the iguana. "Need to stop doing that. I am not a reptile person. Got it?" I shot down the square stairwell in my T-shirt and bare legs and looked through the peephole.

Evan was there, peering through the windows.

I cracked open the door, hiding behind it. "Yes? Is there anyone else with you?"

"Just me." No flirting. No checking out to see what I was—or wasn't—wearing. Just concern all over his face. "You okay? I heard a scream while sitting out here."

"Why were you sitting out here?"

"Waiting for you to wake up."

"Oh." Stepping back, I let him in. "You were waiting for me to wake up?" I realized I now had no door to hide behind, and Evan was looking at me in my sleeping shirt. Why couldn't I stay dressed around him?

"Well, yeah, ever since that first day, I don't come in anymore without making sure you're awake. I sit right there." He pointed to the old wrought iron bench underneath the front window. "Good time to have my coffee."

"I didn't know you did that." That was sweet of him.

"I usually wait until you're dressed, too, but I'm okay with this." He eyed my bare legs sticking out underneath the shirt. "Really okay with it." His deep brown eyes flared, and I felt a sincerity emanating off him that I hadn't before. No, this man wasn't simply making an older woman feel good about herself, and he wasn't blowing smoke up my ass. He was honest-to-God attracted to me. I'd been too slow, and too scared, before to see it.

I should go upstairs and change.

The words formed on my lips, but I couldn't say them aloud. In my dream, Josephine Berry had explained how it was okay to dance for men. She was okay with her body, with her sexuality, with the way she chose to live her life, despite what others thought. So, if a woman from 100 years ago, a woman who society had a problem with because of her skin color, could look *me* in the eye and tell me she was confident with herself during an era that made it difficult as hell for women in this country, especially single mothers, then I could be okay with what I wanted—which was Evan.

No denying it anymore, nor should I.

"Do you mean that?" There was a waver, and maybe some desperation, in my voice.

Evan stared at me, lips barely parted, testing the electricity and energy in the air between us, scanning the authenticity in my face, the need for connection in my body. Setting down his toolkit next to the stairs, he said, "Hell, yes, I do." He waited for me to confirm that I felt the same.

I'd never done this before. I'd never abandoned all protocol and went for something I wanted without thinking about it, without analyzing it to death. I could hardly breathe; I was so hinged on his next move. "I'm ready," I barely whispered. "Right now…"

I couldn't believe the words coming out of my mouth.

His dark lashes batted, as his eyes filled with lust, then his thick hands reached out and wrapped around my face, softly but with raw power, and tugged me toward him. I gave into, without question, the hottest, knee-buckling, wall-smashing, deep throaty kiss anyone had ever given me in all my life. Out tongues twisted, as heat and flames and thirst of all colors shot through my body, consuming me like a hot flash, a delicious one that opened me up.

Holy shit.

I'd felt *close* to this way before, a long time ago, when I first met Nathan, but not since we married. Not since I got to know him for who he was, since before it was too late. This burning, aching, irrational need, the kind no one could resist—least of all the robotic, law-abiding part of my brain—tried warning me to stop, because of Nathan, because of God, because of bullshit technicalities, and—

No.

Leave me alone, I commanded before any disparaging remarks about my age or body could roll through my head like bombs, potentially obliterating what little happiness I'd carved out for myself.

Because *I* wanted this.

I needed this.

Probably more than I'd ever needed anything. I didn't care that I'd only known Evan one week. I trusted him. He wanted me, and I wanted him, and we were two consenting adults. There was no problem.

It wasn't long before Evan's searching hands explored my body, and mine pulled up his shirt, felt his abs (he actually had abs), and his delectable, perfect mouth slid along my neck, repairing every dead and broken nerve ending in my body with just his touch. Where would we go? Here, the stairs? I didn't care.

Thank goodness he was strong, because those beastly arms were the only thing holding me up. I'd gone boneless. And then, because my life in Skeleton Key was shaping up weird and magical and terrifying all at the same time, he lifted me and carried me upstairs, like they do in movies, and I tucked my face into his neck to smell the salty overtones of his spicy skin.

"You've got the only A/C," he laughed, explaining why he was carrying me to my room.

"Smart." I laughed, too, because this wasn't just any sex, this was Florida sex, and making sure we were comfortable during a hundred-degree summer was important.

I thought it'd feel strange being with a new man after so many years, especially one younger than me by a few years, who looked like he should have his own TV show. But it wasn't. Not in the least. Being with Evan felt like I'd known him a long time, like we'd been friends forever, but it wouldn't have mattered if I'd just met him today—pheromones were at play, and that was okay.

From the second he lay me down on the bed to the moment he lifted my shirt over my head, to the moment when he kissed every inch of my body, savoring every instant, I thought I would internally combust. I ached for more, and he knew it.

I wanted to feel him inside of me. Point blank.

I wanted to wake up, be reminded of who I was, of the woman dormant inside me. The woman who used to feel, who wanted to love and be loved in return, who wanted to be adored, admired. To have, like Josephine Berry, men hopping on trains and traveling miles to see her, no roses or chocolates necessary.

11

My first trip out of the house—a walk down Overseas Highway to a local bakery. Lily's welcome party was tonight, and even though I was the guest of honor, my Nana didn't raise me to come to a shindig empty-handed. It'd been so difficult choosing the right treat to take, however. Everything looked so fresh, tropical, and delicious. Knowing Lily, there'd be tons of awe-inspiring desserts already, so I chose a coconut cream pie, in honor of my street.

It looked so divine!

Walking back, the western sky was neon purple, infused with swirls of orange and strawberry cotton candy. So beautiful, I had to take a picture and send it to my girls. *Not as beautiful as you both,* I texted, *but still lovely. Miss you.* I was nervous. Didn't know what to expect, how many people Lily had invited, or whether Evan would be there.

Evan.

Yesterday had been freakin' intense. Once I made it clear I did not need soft and pretty sex, that I wanted it hard enough to wake me from the dead limbo inside of me, he hadn't held back. And holy coconuts, I might've fallen for him were it not for remembering what love had done to me last time. I would be more careful from now on. Still, keeping my heart out of the equation would be difficult considering how well Evan had listened to what I asked for.

Would he be at the party?

Lily's house loomed up ahead, a black and green gingerbread goth-mare against an eggplant sky. What a beautiful renovation. I knew, without a doubt, that the Berry House would turn out gorgeous as well, regardless of whether or not she decided to keep it. Hopping up the steps, I could hear the festivities happening within, the laughter, the clink of wine glasses and silverware. I allowed myself one last minute of quietude before becoming the center of attention.

Hovering at the door, however, I became distinctly aware of something touching the tops of my sandaled feet. I kicked, dislodging whatever mosquito or dragonfly had decided to flit around my ankles, but something else was there, something made of soft gray light and golden eyes, blinking up and meowing.

"Luna?" My mouth hung open, as I watched the kitty weave a circle-eight around my ankles, turn then disappear through the door.

Which opened with a blast of cheers.

"There she is!" Heloise welcomed me with wide caftan-draped arms. "Come on in, sweetheart. Look who's here, everybody!"

A cat—a ghost cat—had just been here. I'd seen her. Lily wasn't crazy, after all. Well, she was, the good kind of crazy, but Luna wasn't a gimmick invented for TV entertainment as I honestly believed. She existed. That, or I was losing my mind the longer I lived here.

A crowd gathered in the foyer to welcome me in. Jax was there, tipping his captain's hat, Jeanine lifting a wine glass in the air in salute, Salty Sid, way in the back, waving at me, and lots of other people in between. Some I recognized as neighbors from other streets, like Nanette, and some were production crew members from the show—boom operators, cameramen, makeup artists who'd fallen in love with the Florida Keys and decided to rent nearby between seasons.

And then, there was Lily, my personal role model and hero, wearing a light chiffon green and yellow wrap, nutmeg locks twisted into a bun, long beady earrings dangling from her lobes. She handed me a glass of wine. "Everyone, I want you to meet the newest member of our crew, Katja Miller. She's working through the new house, cleaning it up and getting it ready for what I hope will be Season 2. Everyone say hello!"

"HELLO, KATJA!" Fifteen or so people chorused all at once.

"Hi, nice to meet everyone!" I handed the coconut cream pie to Heloise.

"Ooo. Tropic Café is one of my favorite bakeries! I'll set it up at the spread." She whisked it away, as I slowly made my way through the house with the spooky, gothic Victorian interior toward the back where the sliding glass doors were wide open. A three-quarter moon hung over obsidian waters, highlighting silver ripples, as soft waves lapped the shore. "So beautiful," I murmured.

"The goddess smiles at you," Jeanine said next to me, patting my arm. "Glad you arrived. I was starving."

"Don't mind me! Go ahead and eat."

"I'm messing with you. Been noshing for an hour. I don't wait 'til Lily Pulitzer food gets cold. Someone wants to say hello." She slunk off.

I looked down and saw Lily's kitty, Bowie, again with the one-green, one-blue eyes. "Mr. Handsome!" I squealed, squatting to scratch him behind the ears. "You are so beautiful, you know that?"

He knew that.

"I know Luna was here before you, but personally, I love you more. Shh, don't tell her."

Bowie flipped onto his back, so I could rub his belly.

I'd never felt so present or welcomed before, even by this cat. How was it that people I'd never met felt more like family to me than a townful of folks I'd known half my life?

"I hear you're sifting through the new house." I looked up to find a young woman a little older than my daughter was speaking to me. "Find any good props? I fixed up the props in this house. That one…" She pointed to an iron cauldron sitting on a shelf with a skull on it. "And that one." She pointed to a bat made of stained glass hanging in a corner, overlooking the living room.

"Those are amazing! Nothing like that so far. Mostly fabrics, costume boas, that sort of thing."

"Which makes sense, because it used to be a theater long time ago, right?"

"That's what I've been told." I stood to greet her.

"I'm Caitlyn, by the way. Nice to meet you." We shook hands. "I can't imagine being in Lily's shoes."

"What do you mean?" I asked.

"Just having to decide what to do with the property, whether to sell it and put the money into expanding this house, or building on the one you're in currently." She reached for canapes on a coffee table and offered me one. Tasted like crabmeat fireworks and dreams.

"True," I said. "She did say those were her choices."

"Yes, but also, making the decision before the execs arrive."

"Execs?"

"The network people. They'll be here in a month to see it in person. She's hoping to have a tight sales pitch put together by then, to convince them to extend our show to a 2nd season or start a spinoff at the other house. *Witch of Key Lime Lane* has really taken off."

"Yes. It's in the Top 10 of this year, isn't it?" I asked.

"It's the *Cooking Network*'s top-rated show, so they're looking to expand, but you get the unenviable task of helping Lily sift through stuff to figure out its personality."

I nodded. I wondered why, if this house made or break her next TV deal, wasn't Lily there every day, sorting through the house herself. Not that I minded doing it.

"Anyway, I've got to run. Meeting a few friends at the Tiki Bar. Good luck with the house!" Caitlyn ran off. I scanned the room for anyone else I recognized and saw Sid sidling up to me, beer bottle in hand.

"How's it hangin'?" He pulled on the brim of his *Booty Hunter* baseball hat.

"Hangin' great. How's yours doing?" I giggled.

"Oh, you know. An ol' sea dog like me can't complain. I still have it, even if it hangs low. Wait, what are we talking about again?" He hung his chin and wheezed out a laugh.

"I don't know. You tell me."

"Probably better if I don't," he laughed.

"By the way…" I turned to him. "Remember you told me about that wall that used to connect to an old theater? Do you know if it was inside a closet?"

Sid narrowed his crystal blue eyes. "Not sure. I think it was the whole south bedroom wall. Used to be a child's room, and on the other side was the back wall of the theater. It'd have been a teeny theater, though."

Oh, I know, I almost said. I saw it.

"A child's room?" I thought of the dolls, tea sets, and the strange feeling I'd had in my dream that my feet hadn't been my own.

"Josephine Berry, the burlesque dancer, had a daughter—a little girl of about eight or nine. The historical society that commemorated the distillery right here…" He pointed to the side of Lily's house where the famous distillery had been discovered last year by Lily and Jax. "They told us that Josephine and her daughter died in the fire caused by a hurricane that year. What remains is the house, which was later expanded."

"That's so sad," I said.

I thought about the blue light in the stairwell, the one that had led me upstairs. I hadn't believed in ghosts before, but I'd just seen a ghost cat on the doorstep, and I'd never seen balls of energy floating around either, so I couldn't deny their existence either. Could the blue light be Josephine?

"The other day you told me you had your theories on the theater fire," I said to Sid.

"Well..." He rubbed the back of his neck. "It's just that Ms. Josephine was...you know..."

"Black?"

"Yes, from Barbados, I believe. And people didn't treat people of color too kindly in those times. People don't treat people of color too kindly in our times either." Sid shook his head and stared at the moon. "Sometimes I wonder which times are worse."

Someone had walked through the front door, and a quick glance told me it was Nanette, saying hello to everyone in the room like a politician. Behind her, then, appeared a familiar face, dark blond hair, deep set brown eyes, nervously scanning the room...

Evan, whose last name I didn't know, though I'd slept with him yesterday, might've been grinning and greeting the other party guests, but I could tell he was looking for me.

I faced Sid again. "Could you excuse me?"

"No worries. You have fun with that young carpenter, girl. No judgment from me or anyone. I'll be here. Musing."

I stared at Sid facing the ocean under some hypnotic trance. How did he know about Evan? I left the fisherman to his beer and lunar contemplation and whirled around, ready to face the inevitable when Evan's chest met my gaze. I looked up into his soulful eyes. "Oh, hello. Fancy meeting you here." I tried sounding normal, not like I'd had sex with him.

Or like his mere presence made my body liquify.

For a split second, I considered the worst with Evan. Would he pretend like nothing happened? Would his interest in me be over and done with? Worst of all— would he introduce me to a girlfriend or wife?

Stop, Katja, Nana's voice nagged. *The boy likes you. Ever thought of that? That a man might fancy you?*

"Hello, hot stuff. And I mean, wow…hot stuff. Woo!" He bit his lip and gave me a polite hug, which I appreciated because I did not want for anyone— especially Lily—to notice anything between us.

"About that. Can I talk to you a second?" I slunk past Sid, Evan trailing nonchalantly behind me. Down the steps, my sandaled feet sank into sand heated by the day's rays of sun.

"A secret meeting?" Evan cooed. "I likey."

I turned to him, doing my best to wear a business-casual smile for anyone who might be closely watching. I knew what small towns were like and didn't want the gossip to begin.

"This is so weird…for me," I said, remembering how he'd snuck out early this morning while I was still half asleep. "I don't even know what to say."

"You don't have to say anything, Kat."

Kat. I loved that. "Well, it's just…we should probably talk about what happened. I wasn't expecting it, and I certainly wasn't looking for it. If the whole thing seemed unprofessional to you, I am so, so sorry."

"Umm." He glanced back, raised a hand in greeting to a crew member, then turned back. "Listen, it's totally, completely fine. Let me ask you something— did you want it?"

My neck flushed suddenly. Flashes of skin and muscle raced through my mind. "Well, yes…"

"Good, so did I. I think you know that. I'm single, and you're…single, I hope?"

That was the thing. I was mostly single. Just needed a final signature from Nathan and his lawyer, and all would be done. But now that Nathan wanted to get back with me, would I even get the papers?

"Separated. Almost divorced, yes."

"Okay, then." Evan shrugged casually but looked at me with deep intention. "Then it's all good. Nothing's going to change. Last night was amazing, wasn't it?" He cocked his head and smiled.

I nodded, finally letting loose a smile and a sigh. I didn't know how to navigate this. I'd never had sex with anyone I wasn't married to before. How did people do this?

"I had a super-fun time. You had a super-fun time. I think?" He looked into my eyes, through my eyes.

"I did." I bit my smile.

"Good. And we're friends, and I'm still going to come over and work on the house, and see you, and pester you…"

"You don't pester me," I said. "I appreciate having you there every day. I don't feel so alone." Suddenly, there were tears perched on the edges of my lower lids. I felt so vulnerable, but Evan was so sweet about it.

"Hey. Look at me. You're not alone. Okay?" He gave me a hug, longer than any coworkers would give each other, but I didn't care anymore. Everyone was so kind and understanding here, no one would judge if they knew the truth. "I'm here, Sid's here, Nanette's here. And if you want to get together again, I'm game, and if you don't want to get together again, I respect that. Got it?"

I wiped tears facing the ocean, so no one would see them. "I appreciate that so much."

"Of course. No expectations here. None at all. You're a free woman who does as she pleases, Kat. Me, I'm just a court jester, knocking down walls, hoping I land a bigger job with the head honcho over there." He nudged his chin at Lily.

Ah, so he was hoping for more renovation work. I remembered his sketches inside the toolbox, how beautiful they were. I nodded. "Thanks, Evan. As long as we're good."

"We *are* good. We are *so* good." He walked up two steps toward the patio and held out his hand. "Come on, let's get back before people start talking. Not that I mind. Do you see me minding?" His dimpled smile rendered me boneless. My knees weakened, as more images from last night filtered into my brain. His wide, capable hands. The tattoo of a sun and moon over his heart. Glistening, sweaty body, pounding into me like I'd asked him to.

Geez, Louise.

I accepted his offered hand and climbed back up to the house, then I ate and drank to my heart's content, forgetting my troubles, forgetting what little money I had in the bank, forgetting Nathan, as Evan's lingering words glittered in my head—*You're a free woman who does what she pleases.*

12

Three weeks.

That was how long it'd been since I first arrived, and since then, I'd sifted through boxes, organized half the junk, and helped Evan gut half the kitchen. That was fun, throwing a sledgehammer around, kicking in old cabinet doors. Really great way to get out my frustrations. I'd also helped him knock down a wall and gotten to know three other workers who'd joined the demolition crew. All were cute in their own way, but none like him. Evan was a whole 'nother level of sexy.

Nothing more happened in the bedroom between us in the week since he'd slept over, but I was also on a very heavy period and was giving off don't-touch-me vibes. Also, I'd started walking every morning instead of jumping for the coffee machine. How many people could say they had a beach right outside their house? I couldn't waste the opportunity and walked forty-five minutes every morning.

Today, I was coming back up the slope toward the back patio, loving the activity surrounding the house—the men hammering, carrying pieces of broken drywall away, installing new drywall, plastering—when I paused and stared at the house. I could see it—the way it had looked back in Josephine's time. With the turrets, two of the three bedrooms, and a small theater where the third bedroom was. In place of today's men busy working appeared other men, arriving with their valises, bottles of whiskey, and bushy mustaches. All to see Miss Josephine.

Standing in my bedroom window, staring longingly out to sea, was the lady herself, her long dark curls falling over silky shoulders, a kerchief tying up the middle section of hair. Without makeup, she looked like a girl, a child no older than eighteen, and it occurred to me that I was more than twice her age with less life experience, whereas she had a house, a theater, a daughter and a business to call her own. It made me feel like I'd wasted a lot of time being married to Nathan. No regrets being a mother to Hailey and Remy, but I wished I'd advocated more for myself. If only Josephine could know that I admired her determination.

When I squinted away from the morning glare, she was gone. So were her admirers arriving at the theater, but Evan and the house were still there, getting restored to new glories.

In the late afternoon, I'd finally gotten rid of half the boxes in the bedrooms and had set aside some of the naked dolls to show Lily, when I came back upstairs to realize the dolls were lined up like little soldiers against the wall. Three composite, plaster dolls from the old days, and four plastic, modern ones. In front of each was a teacup, and someone had put a feather in each of their hair.

I should've been shocked, but I'd gotten too used to odd things happening in this house to assume it was Evan, Lily, Nanette, or anyone who walked in on a weekly basis. Someone was living in the Berry House with me; I didn't mind, and I was no one to tell her it was time to go. I picked up one of the older dolls and ran my fingers over her composite, clunky body.

"Maybe somebody would like a new dress for their dolly?" I asked aloud. I waited for a reply, as if someone might whole-heartedly agree.

Picking up the three oldest dolls, one of the plastic ones, and two bolts of fabric under my arm, I headed downstairs, passed Evan getting water from the cooler, and announced, "Be right back."

He paused chugging for a gulp of air. "Counting on it."

I smiled and headed out, crossing the gravel front yard, thinking how much I loved having a friend with benefits. In 44 years, I'd never known what that was like. I walked up to Nanette's house and turned past her white picket fence, splitting through her perfectly manicured front lawn decorated with palm trees, bromeliads, and wild orchids growing everywhere.

I knocked and waited, glancing back at the Berry House. Evan, cutting a piece of wood with his circular saw on the front patio, had removed his shirt and tucked it into his back pocket. Holy toolkit, I'd slept with that man? Me? This twenty-five-pounds-overweight older woman with arms like bat wings and thighs of butter?

Lucky duck, Nana said.

"Nana!" I scolded, right as Nanette opened the door.

107

"Katja, I don't generally like the nickname Nana, but I'll accept it, only because you're new, and sweet, and I feel sorry for you."

I winced. Last thing I wanted was having anyone feel sorry for me. "Thank you, I think."

"What do you have there? Bolts of fabric?"

"Yes, some of the ones I found in the trunks. I've been trying to decide what to do with them, and now I have an idea."

"Oh? Do tell. Come in." She made way for me, closed the door, then led me to an open, airy room in the back filled with perfectly even rows of storage boxes and craft stuff.

"I want to make dresses for these dolls, like the ones I used to make for my girls when they were little. Are there any you would like before I cut into them?" I set the bolts down on a large, white table with a yardstick for trim. Next to it was the sewing machine she'd mentioned. It was a nice one.

"I would say yes, but here's the truth—I don't have time to sew. I have a mahjong game to get to in ten minutes, otherwise they'll start without me, and I'll lose the $50 I've put in."

"You put money in to play mahjong?" I asked, wishing I had fifty random dollars to gamble for entertainment.

"What's the point, otherwise?"

I had no answer for that.

"But you can stay, look through my boxes. If you see anything you like, go ahead and use it. Unless it's gold lamé, which I use for table runners for the holidays, but anything else, go ahead and use. I've got to run, Katja."

"Can I mess with your sewing machine, see if I can get it running?"

"By all means, dear. Work your magic. I'm all out of it. Lock the door behind me. See you soon."

"Thanks, Nanette." I watched her leave then turned to the higher-end model Singer and sat at a padded chair. The first thing I noticed was that her needle was bent. That probably jammed the machine itself, so I removed that and set it aside, removed the last bobbin used, then the throat plate. Underneath was a major tangle, and I used a pair of scissors to cut the nest of threads and throw it all away underneath the sewing table.

Easy fix. She could've done it herself.

Rummaging through her boxes for wherever she kept the new needles, I got the distinct sensation that air had been displaced behind me. Someone was watching. I looked over my shoulder, spotted no one, then went back to searching Nanette's immaculate cabinet of drawers. The woman enjoyed organizing her crafting and sewing materials more than she actually used them. I found countless zippers, pattern weights, buttons, and dozens of other things still in their brand-new packages.

"She doesn't use any of them."

I whirled around to find the purple-haired kid watching me from the hallway. "Goodness. You scared me."

"Sorry. Need help?"

"Uh…sure," I said. "Even though I don't know what I'm going to make yet."

"But you're going to make something with those dolls, right?"

"Probably."

"Can I see them?"

"Of course." I lifted one of the vintage dolls and held it out like a slice of ham to a shy kitty. "Here you go."

The lanky teen emerged from the dark hallway. Feminine energy with boyish clothes, small breasts that I had a feeling were being bound underneath the baggy clothing. "I'm Sam. He/him," the teen said without getting too close.

"Katja. She/her." I'd never introduced myself using pronouns before and I felt ultra-modern and woke. Hey, whatever got this kid out of the dark and into the light where he belonged. I was thrilled he wanted to make something with me.

"What are these made of?" Sam flipped one of the dolls over and checked the undercarriage.

"Sawdust and glue, a composition that's shaped into the body and head. That's how they used to make them a long time ago."

"Are you going to redo the faces?" he asked.

"Not sure. I guess it'd make sense if I'm going to give them new clothes. I was thinking Victorian gothic, something that could match Lily Autumn's house, in case she likes it."

"This is for her?" He held up the doll.

"I don't know yet. Why don't you help me design them, then we'll decide what to do with them? We'll just have fun."

"I can paint faces, if you want, while you make the clothes. I was in drama three years, did most of the cast's makeup. Can do them in a creepy, but beautiful style. I do my own makeup. Want to see?"

"Sure!" I leaned in, as Sam pulled out his phone and thumbed through TikTok showing me his profile where he painted his face in all kinds of delish ways. Clown faces, needle teeth, prosthetics… "Oh, my God! You are so talented. Seriously. You do this for a living?"

He shook his head, hair flopping in his bright green eyes. "Nah, I just post them online. You think they're good? I've got a whole sketchbook of ideas."

In this child, I saw myself at his age—unsure of my talents, undecided, and a bit unmotivated. I, however, kept waiting for a prince to rescue me from my boredom. Sam was still young enough to rescue himself.

"I think they're amazing." I smiled.

He handed me back the composition doll. "Maybe we shouldn't experiment on the old ones," he said. "In case we fuck it up."

"Oh." I was momentarily shocked by the blunt language. "Good idea."

"I'll be right back." He skittered off, hopping around a sofa and bounding into his room. When he returned, he flipped through his sketchbook, and I couldn't believe the sheer, unfair skills of this kid.

"Sam, those are beautiful." His sketches were rough but had clear vision. "What are you going to do with this talent?"

He shrugged. "Other artists are way better than me."

"No." I held up a finger. "Don't do that. Don't compare yourself to more experienced artists. You're just starting out, and that's not fair. How old are you?"

"Nineteen last month."

"See? You're just beginning. You think every talented artist you see on TikTok started out experienced?" I pressed a fist into my hip. The mom in me was coming out now. "Not even close. They all had to start somewhere."

"I guess." His smirk melted into a semblance of a smile.

"You guess. *Pfft.* So, none of that self-deprecating talk. You hear?" What a fine example I was, always talking shit about myself now telling someone else not to do it. "Here's what I'm thinking…"

I pulled forth the bolt of forest green velvet and lay it on top of the plastic doll, adding a strip of lace as makeshift sleeves, and fishnet stockings over the legs. "Add cute little heels, a feather coming out of a small top hat. What do you think?"

"I like it," Sam said. "Very turn of the 20th century. Theatric as hell."

"Right? I think so, too."

"But the makeup can be modern. Bold lines informed by 50s pinups. Bold but beautiful. I love the gothic aesthetic."

"I do, too! Because you know the house I'm working at used to be a theater, right? So, I thought: what if I make a doll that looks like a burlesque dancer? You think Lily Autumn would like it?"

His emerald eyes flickered with gold flecks in the light coming in through the windows. "Definitely."

"Let's try it and see, shall we?"

For the next couple of hours, we cut the fabric, put the pins in, while I re-threaded the sewing machine, and got a basic draft going. I slipped the shift onto the doll, pleated the sleeves where I wanted, stuck pins in, while Sam sketched face ideas in his notebook, his gangly legs in sweatpants hanging over the edge of the couch.

"Is the house haunted?" he asked.

"Ooo…" I sucked in a breath. "You're treading in tricky waters, kid. I don't believe in the paranormal. And yet, I'm starting to have no choice."

"Why? Because stuff happens?"

I nodded. "You could say that."

"I hear men cheering at night," he said.

I shifted my focus to Sam's face. So, I wasn't the only one.

He went on. "My grandmother says it's the power of suggestion. Because I know it used to be a theater, she says my brain knows what to imagine. It fills in the rest of the information."

Holding the doll up, I saw I was off to a good start, but the dress needed more. A lot more. "Your grandma is Nanette?"

"Thought you knew that."

"I mean, I assumed. Sounds like she's right."

"It's bullshit," Sam muttered resentfully. Where were his parents? Except for that one day at the Berry House, I rarely saw him. He didn't even come to my welcome party.

"Okay, then." I chuckled. "If that's how you feel."

"It's true. That house is haunted as fuck."

113

"Language!" I snorted.

"Sorry. It's haunted as shit."

"Much better. Why do you say that?" I asked.

"Because I've seen her," he said.

I looked back at him over the chair. "Who?"

"The little girl you're making these for. In the front-facing window." Sam looked up and batted his long eyelashes, as my jaw dropped. "She's mixed race—brown hair, light eyes, inquisitive face. And her mother is the one who owned, operated, and starred at the theater. You know all this. You just needed to hear me say it."

13

There were other dancers. Not just Josephine. About eight in total. All young women, none older than twenty, ranging from white to Black to Latina maybe? All I knew was that I watched them from the balcony, as they sat astride their chairs onstage, stockinged legs wide apart, feathers covering their upper torsos, tipping their hats to the male audience. Coins and roses flew into hats, as cheers of admiration filled the theater.

I was dreaming. I had to be. I couldn't remember getting out of bed, walking into the closet, or moving through the portal, yet here I was. I seemed to remember going to sleep early after an exhausting day. After the kid next door hurt my mind by challenging my beliefs, I'd taken melatonin to help me get to sleep faster.

Each of these girls, same age as my daughters, worked their asses off for coin. Part of me applauded them, while part of me wanted to cover them with shawls and give them money for college. Times were different then, sure, but even today, women exploited their beauty to make it through life. The more everything changed, the more it stayed the same.

The back balcony row had a few empty seats, and there, two men in bowler hats with thick mustaches sat dourly ignoring the show, leaning into each other, deep in discussion. Why come out all this way and pay for a ticket if not to cheer the ladies on? I wanted to flick them for being rude. Standing in the shadows, watching the theater erupt into roaring applause, listening to the old-timey music, I again felt like I was observing through a sheet of glass, like my gaze was not my own.

Feet. Look down at your feet.

I wasn't sure who was telling me this, but I did.

Like last time, they were tiny—a child's feet in rich, honey tones and baby soft skin. It wasn't me. I was in someone else's body, standing in the shadows, holding one of the old, composite doll in the crook of my left arm. I glanced at the men, so deep in discussion. I wanted them to pay attention to the show. I didn't care for the way they looked, nor the way they pointed to the ceiling or other areas of the theater, completely in their own world of men's discussions.

I shifted in the shadows, and again, the men noticed me as they had last dream, except this time, they stood from their seats and moved toward me, whites of their eyes focused. "Get her," one said, intent on reaching me, but I knew the secret passageway back to the house, back to my room, and they didn't. Even if they did, they wouldn't fit if they tried.

I didn't know why they wanted to capture me, but I knew they didn't like me or my mother, the star of the show, the reason they'd come. Or was she? Why were they here anyway, if not to watch her performance?

Good thing I was tiny and could outrun, outmaneuver, them. I darted behind the curtain, slipping into a swiveling, wooden door that slammed shut behind me, and hopped over beams and dead mice into the closet, into the safety of my room, the fanciful music from the Victrola fading behind me, the cheers bringing a certain comfort. As long as there were cheers, there was money, and Mama and I could stay...

A boat horn blared in the distance, and I opened my eyes to bright morning sunlight and a humming A/C unit. I wasn't a little girl hiding in the balcony of the theater watching my mother and other women dance. I wasn't running from men upset that I'd seen them, men who wanted to kidnap me, teach me a lesson. I was me, Katja Miller, back in my room, in the strange house where I'd agreed to live and work for Lily Autumn, a TV personality in the current day.

Kidnap...

The word snaked through my mind. Was that what those men wanted? But it wasn't me in the dream. It was Josephine's daughter, the same little girl Nanette's grandson spotted in the window of this house. Either I was having strange dreams of my own, or a little girl's memories, locked in this house, were fusing with mine at night.

I sat up when I caught a flash of green to my right. Iggy, the iguana, was on the floor of my room, rolling his eyeball at me. Did I care, flinch, or scream? No. He was just as much a part of this house as the trunks, boxes, stairs, and walls. If anything, he belonged here more than I did. Unplugging my phone, I braced myself to find new texts from Nathan, even though he couldn't. Even though I'd blocked his ass. But this was the trauma I lived with, fearing that he would somehow contact me anyway. There were only two messages from

Hailey and Remy, nicely reminding me about money for their trip.

I replied, *Will send some now. $$$*

The truth was, I couldn't send much. Most of what I'd made in the last few weeks had gone to unpaid bills, but I could spare a bit for my girls. I wish I'd had the opportunity to go on a weekend trip with friends in college, but I hadn't, so every extra penny I earned, I'd give them so they could enjoy chances I didn't.

"What?" I asked Iggy, still eyeballing me. "What are you looking at?"

Iggy seemed to think that the girls should work for their own money, and while I agreed, they'd have the rest of their lives to work after college, so it was okay for me to give them spending money now. I wouldn't have them forever. "So there," I told Iggy, scoffing at the absurdity of that.

When I slipped back into the room after using the bathroom, Iggy was no longer there, but the bluish light was, pulsating near the floor where the iguana had been standing.

My arm hairs stood on end. Were Iggy and the blue light one and the same? Or were there two entities visiting me? Slowly, I slipped my feet into sandals and stared at the swirling mass of sparking electricity inching its way across the ether into the hall, then made a right and headed for the front-facing bedroom.

Something told me to follow. "Where are we going?" I asked the blue light.

It grew bigger, less concentrated, more faded than glowing, then shrank and grew again in intensity. I got the distinct feeling it was using what little strength it had to show me the way. To where? To the bedroom I'd just spent two weeks organizing? To the closet where I'd pulled out boxes of perfectly modern things left behind for some odd reason?

"What about it? I took all the boxes downstairs," I told the light, laughing, because I was talking to a non-person, possibly even a figment of my imagination. "There's nothing left."

The light led me to a closet. Now that Mount Boxmore was gone, the room was empty, and it was easy to see what I hadn't before. There in the ceiling was a large 3x3-foot door with a chain hanging from the center. Funny the things we could see if we just looked upwards.

"Well, shit. There's an attic."

I pulled on the chain, opening the trap door where a musty smell coughed in my face, and an extendable ladder slipped down an inch then stopped. Grabbing the last rung, I slid the whole thing out until it nearly touched the floor. Of all the items I had to do today, exploring the attic hadn't been one of them, but if more junk was inside, I may as well go through it. That's what I was getting paid for.

Hoisting myself up the rungs, I poked my head into the attic space, one hand in front of my face to safeguard against cobwebs or mice that might decide to jump out at me. Sunlight filtered through two small windows I'd never noticed from the outside of the house. If I'd considered an attic at all, I'd imagined a small crawl space too small for a person to stand, but this attic had plenty of space for standing. It would've made a beautiful bedroom without all the dust.

To my relief, there was nothing in it, except for another trunk way in the back.

"You've gotta be kidding me." Here I thought I could start cleaning the house top to bottom, now that I'd gotten rid of most of the boxes.

I climbed into the space and stood, just barely clearing my head, when again, I saw something green move in my peripheral vision. Iggy sat in the small windowsill, basking in the sunlight. "What the heck?" My mouth hung open. "How did you get up here?" I asked the large lizard, coming all the way up to him.

Nervously, he backed up an inch, unsure what I would do to him. *He* was nervous about *me?* How had he gotten up here so quickly?

"Tell me and be honest," I said, hands on hips. "What are you? A ghost lizard? You can tell me." I glanced at the last trunk against the far wall. "How much you want to make a bet there's more costumes inside of that?"

I marched up to the trunk, an older one by the looks of it, judging from the corroding wood and rusted hinges. Must be difficult being a wooden trunk sitting in pure humidity every day of the year. Lifting the latch, I tried prying open the lid, but it was stuck.

"Put your hip into it," I said, shoving the lid with my enormous ass, the one Evan seemed to appreciate last week. I slammed against the lid again, but it wouldn't budge, and I had no desire to get my untanned hip bruised.

I would have to go downstairs and find the key. Maybe it would finally be useful, although by now, I knew that these trunks would open when they damn well felt like it, not when a key demanded it. I'd been here long enough. I knew the drill. Grabbing the side handle, I swiveled it ninety degrees. Whatever was inside wasn't too heavy. Thank goodness. I lugged it a foot at a time, scraping it along the floor, taking a step, and lugging again, but the more I tried to move it, the heavier it seemed to get.

"Okay, that's weird."

I could understand why the previous owners didn't take the trunks when they moved out. They were a pain in the ass, and forgive me for having odd thoughts, but the trunks themselves didn't seem to want to go anywhere either, as if trunks could have tantrums and refuse to budge. It took all of five, cardio-intense, sweat-releasing, heart-pounding minutes just to lug the darned thing to the attic door where I collapsed in a heap.

From the windowsill, Iggy watched amusedly.

"Now, what?" I'd toss the trunk downstairs? How had this thing even gotten up here? From the looks of it, it wouldn't even fit through the attic trap door. "Stay," I ordered the chest, dropped my feet through the floor, and started coming down the ladder. "Going to find the key. Be right back."

But the moment my feet hit the floor, I heard it—the familiar *clack*, the sound of a trunk unlatching in the space above me.

"You have got to be kidding me." I hung onto the ladder and caught my breath. *I swear to God…*

Don't swear, girl, Nana said inside my head.

"Oh, you be quiet. I'm doing my best here."

Then, another voice…

That's what you get for being out of shape.

121

"Shut. The fuck. Up," I gritted through my teeth at Nathan's intrusive memory.

What kind of loneliness was I living when I spoke aloud to ghosts of my past and silent iguanas and energy balls? Even with all the oddities contained within these walls, none presented a threat so large as the memory of my soon to be ex-husband taunting me when I least needed it.

Sucking in a renewed breath, I climbed up the steps again, poking my head into the attic. Yep, the trunk was open. Wide open. And Iggy was nowhere to be found. What a surprise...not. I scrambled into the attic space again, using the edge of the trunk to help pulley myself up, then looked inside the crate.

More dolls?

Tons of them. At least twenty more. A whole army—white dolls, brown dolls, every color in between. All faded, all severely damaged by humidity. Eyes of all jeweled colors—emerald, amber, sapphire, jasper, tiger's eye. Dull strands of red, black, and blond "hair" hung limply around the faces. Even if I stripped them of their moldy old clothes, I wasn't sure I could save their sawdust and glue bodies. Stuck to the inner walls of the trunk were small, age-worn scraps of paper with handwritten messages on them:

For my dearest Josephine. From your admirer, Bradley.

For Josephine Berry, in lieu of payment.
– H.L. Vineland

Dear J. Berry, in gratitude. – Robert C. Newman

Gifts? Josephine's admirers had given her dolls for currency? Apparently so. I imagined Josephine accepting cash, trinkets of affection, roses, candy, anything they had to offer. Dolls. How did they know to bring dolls? How did they know she wanted them if she'd kept her child a secret?

I picked one up, grazing her eyelashes with my fingertips. *Word of mouth,* the answer came to me, as I set the doll back inside the box. It seemed the more I handled the house's antique items, the more I knew. Why? How could I see into the past so clearly?

Energy remains, something told me.

I picked up another doll, and suddenly, I imagined wayward men, sitting on trains chugging their way down to the Florida islands, away from civilization, away from their families and wives, telling lies of business trips and opportunities for real estate and growth. The truth was they were traveling for a chance to see the famous Josephine Berry and her dancers bare all onstage. I imagined them stealing their daughters' dolls in the night, slipping them out of sleeping poses, stuffing sawdust and glue babies into satchels, toting them as offerings, because other men had told them the theater mistress would accept them as payment, and so they'd gambled…

I set down the doll, turned to go, so I could find a garbage bag in the kitchen to bring back and begin taking the dolls downstairs where I'd evaluate the good ones from the helpless ones, because I knew what to do with them. I'd dress them. Sam would repaint them. And together, we might help Lily come up with a new theme for her new *Dead & Breakfast*, and in the event the network passed on the pitch, we might make a little extra money giving old dolls new life. Either way, for the first time in a long time, I felt excited about something.

I had a plan that went beyond survival.

14

Several days later, carrying three dolls under my arm, I headed downstairs. Today, construction had cranked up to 11. I was about to stop in the kitchen for morning coffee before heading out on my walk, only to find the kitchen gone. Kaput. Cabinets, bye-bye. Dust and debris everywhere.

"Psst!" someone called. I whirled. Evan, his baseball cap set backwards as usual, his toolbelt hanging precariously low on his hips. "Check it out."

"I'm checking," I muttered and shuffled over, following his gaze. God, he smelled good. The wall dividing the two living areas was gone, opening up the space for one mega-room that would look amazing as a Great Room for bed-and-breakfast guests. Assuming Lily would convert the house. "Wow, that looks fantastic! Really gorgeous."

A moment of silence elapsed, as we admired the open space. Then, "I know something more gorgeous," he muttered, casting a hopeful glance my way.

It'd been two weeks since we'd done our "thing," whatever you want to call it, and though at Lily's house, he'd sworn we were just friends and there was no pressure to continue, I kept feeling his lustful gaze on me every day in the hopes that I might invite him back upstairs.

I'd thought about it. One side effect of perimenopause—for me, anyway—seemed to be increased libido. I completely understood why older women were called "cougars," because sometimes I woke up feeling I could eat an entire man in one helping, and today was one of them. I'd settled for morning "alone time" instead. It kept reminding me of the countless times Nathan had wished my libido would've been stronger. Guess who was having the last laugh.

Sucker.

Now I had Evan's deep amber eyes undressing me, a world of unsaids, but I had too much to accomplish today besides doing the construction manager. Upstairs were tons of trash bags to bring down, others to donate, more items set aside for whenever Lily could review them between her hectic travel. In addition, I now had a fire under my butt, a creative spark in my noggin, one I knew wouldn't be quenched until I actually did something about it.

"It appears I don't have a kitchen now," I said, letting that hint snake its way across the space between me and Evan. After all, three weeks was a long time to delay experiencing island cuisine.

Luckily, Evan knew how to take a cue. One of the many things he was good at. "I guess I have no choice other than to take you out to dinner then. As for this morning, I brought doughnuts." He nudged his chin toward the dining room where three boxes sat surrounded by two workers rifling through the sugary dream rings.

"Ah, a man of temptation," I said. I couldn't have doughnuts. Not after I'd worked so hard to lose a few pounds by walking every day.

"Can't have you starving, now, can I? Besides, I'm rather fond of the softness." He craned his neck to give my ass a glance then gave me a wicked smile.

Was he really attempting to keep me plump with doughnuts? Was my cushion good for his push-in? As dead-serious as he was being, I had to laugh at the hilarity. Nathan used to mock my extra pounds. Evan celebrated them. Life was improving.

"No, sir. Starving would be no good." I snickered.

His dimples emerged, and my knees turned to melted wax. Light my wick and watch me catch fire. "When we're done for the day, I'll go home, shower, then come back to get you around seven."

"Sounds divine. See you later." I waited until he'd walked off, so he couldn't see me not partaking of his doughnuts then headed for the door, dolls tucked under my arm.

Outside, I caught my breath, remembering that the woman talking to Evan inside wasn't me. The one who flirted, the one who dropped hints had never been me, though it was becoming me, and I was more than okay with that. It was just a shame I had to fly thousands of miles away from home to become that person.

At Nanette's door, I caught her on the way out, keys in hand. "Oh, Katja, good morning! I see you brought new friends." She lifted one of the doll's faces and shivered. "Goodness gracious."

"Yes, they've seen better days. I hate to ask, but do you have any coffee? My kitchen vanished overnight, and I have no car to find nourishment."

"You poor dear." She stepped aside to let me in. "Raid the kitchen. We have apple coffee cake, oatmeal, and bagels. Let Sam fix something for you, work for her keep. Sam!" Nanette yelled, blowing out my right eardrum. "Make Katja some breakfast, please, my love. She brings you enough offerings as it is!"

"That's okay. I can make my own breakfast. Really, you don't have to—" I felt bad she was making Sam do anything for me, and even worse she was using the wrong pronoun.

"Sam!" Nanette yelled again until a dark sleepyhead materialized in the hallway. "You both have been busy with those dolls," she said with a curious tilt to her head. "Are they for anything in particular?"

I wondered if Nanette was a spy for Lily, if she'd been asked or instructed to keep an eye on me while Lily was gone and report back. What would she tell her? That I'd been playing with dolls this whole time? This was part of my master plan to help Lily, in case she didn't know.

"It's just there's so many of them, your grandson and I thought we'd transform them into something new. Maybe to surprise Lily with. Not sure yet, but until I decide, don't say a peep. Please?"

Nanette cocked her head, glanced over her shoulder, then leaned in close to me. "You know she's my granddaughter, right?"

"I beg your pardon?"

"Sam is…" She mouthed *a girl* in silence. "Thinks she's a boy. Having loads of trouble with her

128

parents. That's why she's living here. I appreciate you spending time with her. Maybe the dolls would be good for her? Anyway…" Nanette stopped whispering the moment Sam crawled closer to us in a very obvious attempt to overhear. "Mahjong in ten minutes. Must go!"

She skipped out to her car, as I ambled in, dumped the dolls onto the kitchen counter, and turned to Sam. "Your grandmother doesn't know?"

"She knows."

"But she doesn't respect it," I said.

"Does it look like it? Nobody does. Not my mom, not my dad… They all think it's a phase. Believe it or not, Nanette is the one giving me the least shit over it. That's why I stay here."

A wave of sadness ebbed over me. "I'm so sorry. That must be so frustrating." I admit it wasn't easy to understand what could feel like an odd trend to older people, like Nanette, but I respected Sam enough to treat him as he wanted, as anyone would want to be treated. "I respect you."

Sam sighed, pulled out a bag of bagels and popped one in the toaster oven. "Thanks. Some people have it worse. I'm not complaining. However," he lifted a finger, "the second I have the chance, I'm out of here."

"Where will you go?"

He shrugged. "I don't know. Austin. Salem. New York?"

"Salem?" I helped get our coffee going. "Interesting."

"It's a very witchy town."

"Oh, trust me, I know. I've always loved the idea of living there myself. My grandmother grew up there before she moved to Dayton. Just not sure I could ever live there. I was raised Christian by my parents, and the whole witch thing doesn't vibe with…"

Whom? My family? All dead. My husband? Soon to be an ex. My girls? They weren't much into religion either and would probably encourage me to go. Who was I holding onto the last scraps of my former life for?

"Yeah, well, I was raised a girl, so…" Sam smiled.

"I got you." If Sam could depart from his upbringing, so could I. If only I was twenty years old again, free to go in any direction I pleased. At forty-four, my options were limited. "Look what I brought." I held up three more composition dolls, explaining how I found another trunk filled with lots more inside. "And I was thinking, maybe…if Lily doesn't want them, we could sell them. Once we fix them up, that is."

His eyes lit up brightly. "Like, on Etsy?"

"Sure, why not? But let's see what Lily thinks first. It's only fair she get first dibs."

"Do you mean you would sell them with *me*?"

"Of course, I would. I don't paint faces, and you don't sew clothes. Clearly, it would be a collaboration. What are your thoughts?"

"Hell yeah, it's an idea. Let me get my paints." He ran off more chipper than a curly-tailed lizard, of which I'd seen many running on the hot sidewalks of Skeleton Key, and I smiled as I sat for a quick breakfast. I loved seeing that kid light up.

Only problem was, I didn't have much time to dedicate to this venture at the moment. I had just

GABRIELLE KEYES

enough time to devise a few prototypes for Lily, then had to get the house in perfectly clean order, or else it wouldn't be ready for the execs' visit. For now, though, it wouldn't hurt to get one doll going.

In the craft room, I sifted through fabrics, looking for something stiff I could use for crinoline. Sam came out with a box full of paints and brushes. "What did you do with the first dress you made?" he asked.

"It's at the house. I consider it practice. But when I saw these in the attic, I couldn't help but feel like these would make an amazing collection."

"Let's start with the newest ones, though," Sam suggested. "I'd hate to mark up the oldest ones. Have you seen the little girl yet?"

He meant the ghost child, the one he'd seen in the window. "No, but I've sensed her." That took a lot to admit. "I don't know. I've had dreams where I'm a little girl looking into the theater from the balcony, but I'm sure those are just dreams."

He pulled out a bottle of what looked like turpentine or acetone and dumped a ton of cotton balls on the table. "Maybe you're channeling her," Sam said. "Like you're in her body. Maybe she's using your dreams to communicate with you."

"Interesting. I hadn't thought of that," I muttered, beginning to cut and pull fabric, shape it into general pieces to start with. I pulled up a chair and prepared to fall into a creative zone.

Sam took one of the newer dolls, soaked the cotton with acetone, then proceeded to wipe clean the flaked paint from the doll's face. "Maybe if you make her a doll that looks like her, she'll come out."

I bristled at the idea. Wasn't sure I wanted a ghost to come out at all.

"You know, she'll materialize," he said. "Maybe this first doll can be for her—for Josephine's daughter. I'll start painting this one, since I know what she looks like." He set down the fair white doll and picked up the slightly darker one instead.

We worked for a couple hours—me, creating a Victorian-inspired dress in black and gold with sash and lace trim, while Sam repainted her skin, added large brown eyes, soft eyebrows, pink blush for cheeks, and a curvy, slightly sexy pouty mouth. By the end of the day, we'd created our nearly-finished first doll, a goth babydoll fit for Wednesday Addams. All she needed was her hair fixed up, which Sam had already started working on.

By the time Nanette returned and kissed Sam on the top of his head, I felt better knowing that Nanette meant well, loved her grandson, even if she didn't understand him, and hoped she'd eventually use the correct pronouns out of love and respect. Also, by that time, I'd found, not only a new endeavor to keep me busy and hopefully earn us a few dollars, but a new friend—albeit a young one.

That evening, I showered, content at the full day's work. I'd managed to throw out tons of bags, which Evan helped me transport to the dump using his truck, I'd set aside a good amount of items for Lily to review, and I'd taken all the remaining dolls to Nanette's house to assess. When the older woman saw how happy the dolls made her grandson, how Sam's face literally lit up like a moonbeam, she allowed the intrusion, even made space for the dolls in the corner of the craft room.

I spent the rest of the day basking in the fact that I'd gotten so much done in one afternoon, had made Sam's day, and was well on my way to showing Lily my new ideas. So she could have a fuller picture, I even sat on the patio an hour sketching what a second *Dead &* *Breakfast* might look like, a creepy dark house with refurbished dolls on every shelf.

When the sun started going down, however, I jumped up and headed to the shower. It was time for dinner with Evan. By then, I was ravenous, not only for a meal out on the town, but for the man himself. Yeah, it was okay, I decided, setting my guilt free and watching it go down the shower drain.

15

Ever gone on a date with the intention of grazing on a light salad to appear delicate as a flower, but you know you're a ruminant buffalo with multiple stomachs? With my kitchen gone and no car of my own, it was all day before I could eat anything other than the bagel Sam made me, and now I was starving.

Evan and I sat al fresco at *Lazy Lobster* with a plethora of dishes between us. He insisted on getting lots of appetizers so I could try a bit of everything, and I was doing my best to decide between the peel-and-eat shrimp, the calamari pasta, and the conch fritters for my next bite. I'd had these fritters before at Lily's beach bonfire, I just hadn't known what they were back then.

"Did you like it?" Evan watched me eat like he was Len, the judge on *Dancing with the Stars*.

"So good. But why am I the only one eating? Are you a vampire?"

"Yes, though I tire of blood and 21st Century food bores me." His antiquated voice impression was sexy. He would make an amazing onscreen vampire.

He laughed his grunt-like laugh and dove his fingers into the mahi bites, plucking one out and dipping it into the garlic butter. When he popped it into his mouth, I never wished so hard to be a mahi bite. He laughed at me.

"What's so funny?" I asked. "Aside from me drooling when you do that?"

"Your honesty, Katja. I love it."

"What do you mean? I haven't laid a shred of honesty on this table tonight."

"But you have. You don't play games. You don't pretend. I'm so used to women who play games. They don't act in accordance with what they're feeling. They play coy instead of saying they want more or act bored when they're interested. Games get old after a while."

Oh. I had no idea what guessing games or dating games were like, since I'd never played. Wasn't everyone supposed to show their true feelings?

"Does that mean I'm supposed to act different?"

"No, it means stay exactly who you are. I really appreciate it." He tipped back a bottle of local beer, allowing me two seconds to check him out, before he set it back down again. With those forearm vein ropes peeking out his folded blue sleeves, I could've jumped into his lap.

"I guess you must date a lot." My eyes cast downward. I hadn't intended for it to sound like a nosy question, but if we were going to be friends, I preferred the transparency.

"I don't."

"That's impossible. You're hotter than a glue gun left on all day at the craft fair, Evan."

He snorted and took another swig of beer. "Holy shit, that's funny." He wiped his chin where beer had dribbled. "I don't date. Most of the women who live in the Keys are either married, or older than seventy."

"What's wrong with older women, Evan? Huh? I thought you liked us." I ribbed him. Of course, he meant senior citizens, not someone in their mid-forties, but I still loved seeing his reaction.

"Nothing at all. I find older women very attractive, especially the ones who haven't given up on their appearance."

"How so?" I raised an eyebrow. "Women don't take care of their appearance for men, Evan. Explain."

He lifted his palms. "You got me there. All I mean is, I've seen women who don't bother with their looks anymore. Maybe they assume life is over. Maybe they never cared about it in the first place. I think at fifty, life's just getting good."

I swallowed softly. "I was one of those women until recently," I confessed. "Still am, if I'm honest."

"No. You're so sure of yourself."

"Me?" I nearly fell off my plastic chair. "I'm really not, Evan. I'm the farthest thing from what you just described. I've been trying out new skin around you, but the truth is, negative shit talk gets to me every day."

"I would never know if from out here."

"It's true, though. This is probably more than you wanted to know about me, but I went through a shitty marriage. And the sad thing is, I didn't even *know* it was a shitty marriage, because I had nothing to compare it to, and because I was so used to the way he talked shit about me."

"Damn. I'm sorry." He held his fork in mid-bite. "And for the record, that's not more than I wanted to know. I've wanted to know more about you for a while now. I just didn't want to look like a creep. Also, I've been keeping my distance, because well…I'm there to work, too. Plus, you need your space."

I nodded. "I appreciate that. I do need space, but I also need to feel good about myself again, which is why we…well…"

The dimples came out to play again. "I get it. Remember the other day at Lily's, I told you it was okay to want both? I'm fine with it, Katja. I really am. But you do intrigue me. I'm not gonna lie."

I do?

I honestly thought that whole speech was so he could continue to date and have sex with as many women as possible. An easy way to keep me at arm's distance. What about me could possibly intrigue him?

"It's my love handles, isn't it?" I asked. "You can't resist them."

He sniffed a laugh. "Yes. And your millions. You should probably know, before we go any further, that I'm a gold digger. Nanette wasn't kidding when she said I was dangerous."

"Well, sir…if love handles and money are what you're after, you should know I only have fifty percent of those. Which fifty percent is up to you to figure out. I can't say anymore."

A quiet laugh bubbled up in his chest until he was red in the cheeks, either from the beer, or my stupid jokes, or the remnants of the dying sunset beaming on him. I looked toward the horizon that was swallowing a ball of flame.

Reality seeped in again. "Evan. Dating is just something I don't think I can't handle right now." Realizing what I was saying, I added, "Says the girl on a date with a gorgeous man. Ugh." I dropped my head in my hands. "You must think I'm an idiot."

"Hey." He reached out to pull my hand away from my face. "Not true. I don't think that, and don't say that about yourself. Look, I get it. You're in a transition period. Nobody needs another relationship when they're figuring out their life. I understand. I've been there. That's why this isn't a date. It's two friends having dinner."

"You've been there?" I rubbed my sexy snot with the back of my hand.

He handed me his napkin. "Yeah. It's been a while. I got married too early. Twenty-one. She was pregnant."

"Oh, no."

"Yep. The baby didn't survive. After that, we didn't last long either."

"I'm so sorry."

He shrugged. "It wasn't meant to be. I only bring this up to tell you that for a long time, I couldn't be with anyone. Then two years ago, I meant a woman while doing a job in Marathon…"

Simply hearing that he'd met a woman made me feel twinges of jealousy I had no right to feel after telling Evan I wasn't interested in a relationship other than "friends with benefits." Still, I nodded and did my best to listen.

"We were together for almost a year." A more somber expression overcame Evan's face, one with forehead lines and tightness around the mouth.

"What happened?" I asked.

"Her husband happened."

"What?"

"Yep." He got lost in thought a moment, then snapped out of it, popping the last mahi piece into his mouth. "Apparently, they were separated. She was in the Keys for distance from him."

"And she said nothing about him?" I asked.

"Nothing. That's why when I say I appreciate your honesty, I mean it, Katja. Thank you." He lifted his beer. "To honesty."

"To honesty." I lifted my beer for a toast. "So, we've both been lied to. To not dating, then!" I was even more glad now we were on the same page.

"To not dating," he echoed. "To not being interested in anyone else while we move onto bigger and better things." Evan clinked his beer bottle with mine.

"Hear, hear. To not needing anyone," I agreed.

"Except for sex," he said, holding up his pointer finger. "As long as we both agree."

"Except for consensual sex." I smiled, but wow— he was nailing us on the head. Except now I felt weird. "Evan, you must think I'm on crack."

"I wouldn't say crack. I'd say strong weed with a few chasers of whiskey." He leaned back and stretched, and I gave him the middle finger. "But that's okay, because so am I."

Believe it or not, that made me feel better.

When he pulled into my driveway, another car was there—a Mazda CX-9. Evan shut off the truck lights and crept in quietly. "You expecting someone?" He parked, as we both climbed out and started up the walk.

That couldn't be Nathan, could it? Maybe he'd rented a car? No way. He had no money to rent a car. My fears were sabotaging my night again.

"No," I said. From the driveway I saw the front door slightly open, but as soon as I heard the voice inside the foyer, I knew who was here. "It's just Lily, back from New York."

Evan stopped in his tracks and backed up a step. "Ahh. Guess I'll…just be going then."

"Wait." I didn't want him to leave just yet. We'd had such a great time, flirted, and hinted at getting together tonight all throughout dinner. Lily wouldn't mind if we'd gone to dinner together, would she?

I knocked on the open door. "Hello?"

"In here, Katja!" Lily called.

I gave Evan a pleading look, but he was already halfway to the car, waving and pointing to his phone, saying he would text me later. I couldn't blame him for wanting to take off before Lily could see him. Not that her hires weren't allowed to have a personal life or anything.

I stepped in. "Hey! Just got back from dinner."

The lady herself was in jeans and a black T-shirt, and I loved that she was starting to look more and more like a normal, everyday person to me instead of a celebrity. "No worries. Sorry if I came in while you were gone."

"No need to explain," I said. "It's your house."

"I know, but you're living here, after all. Anyway, Heloise and I were coming back from dinner ourselves, and we figured we'd stop in and see how things are going. So…how are things going?"

Heloise came in from the back patio. "Did we catch you at a bad time?"

"Not at all," I said, nervously wringing my hands. "To answer your question, things are going well, I think. Just today I threw out tons of bags, and I have a whole corner of items for you to look at upstairs."

"May I?" Lily pointed up the stairwell.

"Of course. Come." I led them up the stairs. Showing her my progress always made me nervous, considering how soon she wanted the house to be ready, like no matter how much work I did, it would never be clean in time.

Lily and Heloise followed me into the second bedroom, the one where I'd lined up items against a wall. "You can see I've gotten rid of a lot of boxes."

"Yeah, you have!" Lily seemed pleased. She looked around and opened the closet with the attic door. "Very nice!"

I let out a sigh of relief. "Thanks. Oh, and I don't know if you know this, but there's an attic up there." I pointed to the closet.

"In here?" She looked upwards into the closet. "Oh, wow, you're right. Does it open?"

"It does," I said.

"And?"

"There was another trunk up there," I said, pausing, wondering if to tell her about the dolls, not really having a choice, since anything in the house belonged to her. "There were more dolls up there."

"Really," she stammered.

"Yep. From what I've heard, a little girl used to live here a long time ago. Sid said it, Nanette's grandson said it... Someone from the Florida heritage association also mentioned it, Sid said."

"I think I remember this. Where are they?" Lily looked back at the lineup of odds and ends. "The dolls."

"They're at Nanette's. I just put them there to get them out of the way. I plan on starting to clean tomorrow." The moment I said it, I felt like I was lying. I'd hoped to sew more dresses and work with Sam on the dolls tomorrow.

"Okay, good." She whirled around. "That's what I was hoping. We have a little less than two weeks before Josh and Elaine arrive, our exec friends at the network, and I'm hoping to have the one large room renovated by then and most of it clean."

"It should be done by then. No worries, Lily. Were you thinking I'd be further along by now?" I was wringing my hands so hard, they were burning between my fingers. "Because I can work harder, faster. I don't mind the pressure. In fact, I can—"

"No, it's fine. It's fine," she repeated, shifting across the hall into the other room. I looked at Heloise's face for more clues, but she just nodded and smiled.

"Fine" didn't sound good. In fact, she seemed a bit worried but was clearly giving me the benefit of the doubt. I'd told her I could do anything, so I could not let her down. One way or another, dolls or no dolls, Evan or no Evan, I'd have this house brand-spanking sparkling clean, even with the construction going on.

As Lily checked the other room, I considered whether to tell her about some of my distractions, like the closet that led to another dimension but decided against it. Although I was sure Lily would appreciate a good ghost story, it didn't seem like the right moment to share.

Heloise lifted a bolt of cloth and rubbed her fingers along the velvety smoothness. "I think it's looking great, Katja. Lily, there shouldn't be a problem."

"I know, but Elaine and Josh were a little hesitant at our last meeting. I just want everything to be perfect," she told Heloise.

I didn't know these Elaine and Josh people, but I could see that Lily was under a lot of pressure to impress them.

As if reading my thoughts, she looked at me. "Sorry. See, my ex got another show on another network last month, so now I'm feeling…"

"Like you need to compete?" I said. Or maybe it wasn't my place to say that.

"Yes." Lily nodded hard. "There's a little competitiveness there. I'm trying to work through it. Sorry if I seemed like I was pressuring you. The house was probably more work than I realized when I hired you, and that is definitely not your fault." She smiled.

"I can do it. I can speed it up," I said. "There've been a few setbacks, plus I've been worried about my ex finding me here, and…" Out of nowhere, I felt vulnerable, way more out in the open than I'd intended, but something about these ladies made me feel okay in sharing.

"Oh, honey." Heloise took my hand and patted it. "Anything we can do?"

I dabbed the corners of my eyes. "You already have. You are helping, right now, by letting me be here. Thank you."

Lily grabbed my other hand. "We're going to make sure you get through this, okay?"

We stepped out of the room, and they headed for the stairs, but from where I stood, I caught a glimpse of the inside of my room. I'd left the bedside lamp on, and the doll vaguely resembling Josephine's little girl was on my bed with a teacup set in front of her.

I gasped.

Lily looked back at me. "You okay?"

"Fine," I said, glancing at the doll again, her eyebrow high, lips black and pouty. Despite being a little freaky, I knew whoever had put her there was just hoping I'd play.

"I'll be back in a few days," Lily was saying on her way out. "If you need or want anyone to help you, just say the word, and I'll send more crew to help. I don't want to step on your toes if you got this."

"I got this. I definitely got this," I said. More crew would've gotten the job done faster, but it wouldn't have allowed me the space to think.

Heloise nodded with a slow blink, like she had no doubt I'd get the job done. Her presence was a huge reassurance for me. But it was Lily I had to impress, and it dawned on me that maybe she'd been testing me out this whole time. Like, if I did a good enough job, she'd

144

hire me for more work. Part of me loved the idea of hanging around longer with the *Witch of Key Lime Lane* people, but part of me was terrified of delving further into change.

It was one thing for my job here to be temporary and another to consider never going back to Ohio. Was I afraid of success or of failure?

I waited, hoping for Nana's voice to help me out on this one, but she was uncharacteristically silent. As the ladies left and I waved goodbye, watching the full moon rise in the western sky, I got the sense that I still wasn't alone. And when I turned around, a beautiful little girl was standing there.

16

I sucked in a gasp. I stared.

At the blue-toned child in front of me.

A smiling, delicate creature with bouncy dark curls, eyes like a spring morning, and an old lacy dress with vertical pin stripes.

She hadn't been there a minute ago, or we all would've seen her. She wasn't all there either—only the top half of her body was visible. The bottom half, from the knees down, was gone. Yet, my mind told me she was wearing white stockings. She launched up the stairs, invisible footsteps making a clomping sound, as she giggled and checked over her shoulder to see if I was chasing her.

At first, I couldn't move. I stood rooted, frozen to my spot. What was she? The result of my mind playing tricks? The brain was a fascinating organ, full of firing synapses and mazes of half-truths all trying to connect. To reason. Make sense of all we were too tiny in this universe to understand. But then, reason returned, and I remembered all that had happened in this house in the four weeks I'd been here. The little girl wasn't any different than the blue light, the dolls that moved, the ghost iguana, or the portal into another dimension through the closet. I was just surprised to see her, that was all.

GABRIELLE KEYES

Just a little girl, hoping I'd play with her.

Once the goosebumps on my arms melted away, I sprang up the stairs after her, watching the edges of her dress trail behind, as she slipped into the room with the attic door in the closet. "Wait!" I called. She moved too quickly for me to catch up to her, like hiccups in time moving forward, and I desperately wanted to talk to her. "Who are you? Come back. Please."

Callie.

"Callie?" I said, though I couldn't have known that, because she hadn't actually spoken.

Yes.

She floated through the closed closet doors, dissipating right through them. When I opened them, hoping to find her there, crouched and giggling, there was no one. Not a single soul. The closet was completely empty, except for the chain dangling from the attic door. Maybe she'd entered the attic?

I flicked on the closet light and tugged the chain until the square door creaked open, and the ladder slid an inch, enough for me to extend the whole thing down. Quickly, I went up, rising into the humid murkiness, my breath loud and panting in my ears. I scanned for the little girl but saw nothing but dust motes swirling in the trapezoid of closet light perforating the gloom.

I felt like I was going crazy.

"Callie?" My voice sounded loud in the quietude, heavily dense compared to what I'd just seen and heard—whispers lighter than air. I thought I heard her giggle from another place and time. "I can hear you," I said.

Half my body stuck into the attic, while the other half waited without moving a muscle. I stood, still as a statue, every nerve of my being on high alert, expecting the return of the little wisp of light. When she didn't materialize, I climbed the last steps, scrambled to a standing position, and waited again. Outside, rain clouds were brewing, and a cool breeze hit the attic walls, causing a whistling coo to filter through the gaps in the siding.

The trunk…

"The trunk?"

Whether it was Nana's voice or my own intuition or Callie's or my own didn't matter. What mattered, what I knew in my soul, was that something waited for me there. Something I hadn't seen when I'd taken out the dolls, something faded and sitting at the bottom of the trunk, blending in with the wood and fabrics. I'd seen so many rolled-up bolts in the last weeks, I hadn't paused to consider this one.

Stepping up to the trunk, I peered inside. Underneath articles of baby doll clothing were folded sheets of large, yellow-stained paper. Nervously, I reached in and lifted them out to unfold them. In the dim light, it was hard to read, but the ink was blue, the lines perfectly straight, and the drawing was of a house. Architectural plans. Old ones. Of a house that looked a lot like this one but without the patios, front or back. But with a connecting theater. Drafted in 1924 by Lester B. Weston.

How long had these been around?

Clearly, almost a hundred years just sitting here in the attic all this time. The previous owners really did

148

leave everything behind. Why wouldn't they have taken it, including these plans, which must've been fairly valuable? The more I thought about it, the more I figured they must've left in a hurry. They must've gotten spooked or decided the house was more than they could handle. Had they been haunted by the same visions I'd seen? Had they seen Callie?

Suddenly, I smelled smoke. I ran to the window and tried searching through the dingy glass for signs of fire in the neighborhood, but the discoloration was too thick. Architectural drawings under my arm, I left the attic, jumped to the bare floor, and ran downstairs, depositing the plans on top of an upside-down box serving as a mock table before running outside. Standing on the beach, I scanned the shore for fire.

Nothing.

No orange glow, no smoke pluming into the sky, and no scent of fire. The smell had been a phantom one, and there was no denying now, considering everything I'd experienced in the last month, that I was becoming receptive to otherworldly phenomena.

Sensitive.

Downright psychic.

And from somewhere in the depths of my soul, I heard my Nana say, *About damn time you noticed.*

In the morning, the sounds of men hammering woke me up bright and early. I could count on Evan's crew better than I could my own phone alarm. Slowly, last night's events dawned on me, and I hurried to get dressed so I could show Evan my find. When I got downstairs, I found him already sweaty from climbing up and down a ladder, blond hairs of his muscular forearms illuminated by dust and sunshine.

"Check it out…" I unfolded the plans and presented them to him atop the box I'd laid them on last night.

He studied them, eyes scanning the faded pages. "What you got there?"

"I think they're plans to the house. Right? Doesn't this look like my bedroom here, the kitchen here, and this, the theater?" I pointed out the different areas, waiting for Evan to be impressed. "Am I wrong?"

He took the sheets from my hands and moved them to brighter patch of light near the back patio. "No, I think you might've found something. Where were these?"

"The attic."

"They're in terrible shape. Have you shown Lily?"

"I just found them last night after she left. I had a visitor. A little girl who wanted me to follow her."

He cocked his head at me, a slow smile spreading on his face. "You're shitting me. You saw a ghost?"

"I shit you not," I said. "And I guess so? You know how you were always hearing trunks opening and closing? Well, I think it's her doing it. And guess what? Nanette's grandson, Sam, and I think she's Josephine Berry's daughter."

"Josephine Berry didn't have a daughter. Not that I know of." He wiped his sweat with his short sleeve.

"We think she did, Evan. And she used to hide her in the attic from her patrons because she didn't want anything sullying her reputation as a burlesque dancer. Mothers are not exactly sexy, you know?"

His gaze roved me over. "I wouldn't say that."

"I mean, in those times. Her clientele must've preferred to think of her as young, single, and available. Enhances their desire for her. It would make sense why I've found so many dolls. I'm going to go let Lily know."

Taking the plans from him, I turned. "That's pretty freakin' cool, Kat. They should have those appraised, then put on display."

"They should!" I bolted out the door but didn't get very far when I spotted Captain Jax coming up the steps, waving in a kind of regrettable greeting. "Oh…hi," I said.

"Hey. Can I talk to you a minute?"

"Of course, what's up?" I could sense Evan still lingering nearby, curious to know why Jax was here, too, but I closed the door gently.

Jax took off his signature captain's hat and ran a hand through his hair. "This'll sound weird, but I got a super random call from a guy named Nathan?"

My heart stopped. Literally. Blood drained from my face. "Okayyy…"

"He asked if I knew a woman named Katja Miller, but I didn't tell him yes. I didn't know who he was or why he wanted to know."

"I appreciate that." I sat on the bench, whole body shaking. "Did he say why he was calling?"

"He said he was looking for his wife. Said her phone had been disconnected, and she'd left town. He was worried." Jax shook his head. "But…knowing your interview backstory, I figured he was bullshitting."

"He was." I pinched the bridge of my nose. "Wonder why he called you. How did he even get your number?"

"Well, he called the listed number for the charter boat business. He never mentioned my name. I guess he must've figured you were in Skeleton Key then started calling every business on the island until he got to mine. Figuring out how you're here isn't too difficult, is it?"

"My daughters would never tell him," I asserted, even though he didn't ask. I was sure of it. "I might've mentioned to my former employer that I was taking a job, but I don't think I mentioned for whom, or where, specifically."

Jax leaned against a column. "Do you two still share bills? Credit cards? Phone bills? Maybe he's seen calls from your phone to places in the Keys?"

"I haven't used my credit cards. They're maxed out."

"Maybe you had Amazon deliver something here, and he saw that?"

I didn't want to say that I barely had money for anything, let alone making purchases on Amazon, so I just shook my head. "I haven't had to buy anything since Lily pays my groceries, the house, all the bills, everything."

"Hmm…" His mouth was a thin line, as he looked off toward the ocean.

"Only thing I bought with my new debit card was a pie. A coconut cream pie, the one I brought to my welcome party at Lily's house," I said. "But it's my own bank account, not his."

"Would he have access to statements?" Jax asked.

"No, but…" *Ugh.* "He came back to the house a couple of weeks ago. So, he probably got the mail…"

"Which, he of course opened," Jax said.

When he'd left, I thought he was gone. Forever. Honestly never imagined he'd be back and never thought I'd have to protect myself against him. It wasn't until I got here that he started with his insistent texts. By then, it was too late to change my address on bank statements.

"I hate to tell you what to do, but maybe call the police if you're not comfortable with him knowing where you are. Have a restraining order put on him. He's the one who left. He shouldn't be back, snooping around, much less going through your mail. When's the divorce?"

Tears welled up in my eyes. I hated this. Hated not having closure, hated that, even though I'd come to Florida to forget Nathan, he kept finding a way to torture me. "We're waiting on one thing from the lawyer," I said, even though it wasn't true. It was Nathan we were waiting on, and somehow now I doubted he would sign the papers.

"He might be behind that, too." Jax shrugged. "The only other thing he did say right at the end, when he tried confirming where my business location was, 'You in Skeleton Key, right?' I didn't respond. He said, 'That's where that show is. The one my wife likes.' Then, he hung up."

I let the tears flow and felt a hand on my shoulder.

"Hey, it's okay. Evan in there?" Jax asked.

I nodded, got up, and opened the door. Evan was within sight, clearly waiting to see what the issue was.

"Hey, dude." Evan shook hands with Jax. "Everything alright?"

"Should be," Jax replied. "But just in case, can you make sure all the locks on the doors are in full working order? I know we don't usually worry about stuff like that around here, but just to be safe. And if they're not, get new locks put on by the end of the day?

"Yeah. Sure. No problem. What's going on?" Evan asked me.

"Ex problems. I think he's figured out where I am. I don't think he'll drive all the way down here," I said, "but then again, he's crazy and possessive."

"Thanks, man." Jax clapped Evan's shoulder and gave me another wave, as he backed down the steps. "Give me a call if you need anything. You have my number."

"Thank you, Jax," I sniffed. From the inside out, my whole body was shaking with tremors I couldn't control.

Evan squatted beside me. "Do you need me to stay with you tonight? For no reason other than to guard the front door with my brass knuckles?"

I let loose a small chuckle. If Nathan were to show up here and see another man sleeping in the same house as his technical-wife, things would be a thousand times worse. I didn't know what to do, but I knew this was my burden and nobody else's. "I have to deal with this on my own."

17

My mind buzzed with a hundred questions. Would Nathan come looking for me? Would he cause a scene? Would he be pissed? What rights of protection did I have against him? Why did he go so far as to call Jax? Out of worry or because he thought he owned me?

He thinks he owns you, Nana said.

Damn it, Nana. Stop being right all the time.

On the back patio, I sketched as I worried, or worried as I sketched. I needed fresh air and had taken a few days to sit, watch the ocean, and add details to my drawings for Lily. I'd told her she could count on me, and I would not let her down. Though I wasn't much of an artist, I wasn't half bad at conceptualizing my ideas, the one of a house filled with burlesque dolls had been taking on a life of its own.

Down the beach, a familiar bell rang out. Though I didn't need any fish—didn't even have a kitchen—I sure could use Sid's smiling face. Setting my notebook down on the wooden bench, I headed out barefoot on the hot sand to greet him, shielding my eyes from the glare.

"Ahoy!" Waves bobbed his dinghy ten feet from the shore. Today, Sid wore a Bruce Springsteen muscle shirt that showed off wrinkled skin and droopy muscle tone.

"Hey, you!" I watched him jump out, pull his boat up onto the sand, and set his foot atop his battered white cooler. "What have you got today?"

"A baseball bat."

I laughed. "What for?"

"So, you can beat the living shit out of that ex-husband of yours. Who does he think he is, tracking you down when you're trying to live your best damn life? That's what I want to know."

I could've cried. "Good news gets around fast."

"You know how it is, sister." He gazed fiercely at the construction work going on behind me. "This a small island."

"I know. I love it." I plopped on the sand cross-legged and watched the construction, too. Soon, the new living room would be finished. "But I don't want to hurt anyone, Sid, not even Nathan. Believe it or not. He is and always will be my kids' father."

"Blah, blabbity-blah. He's making you feel unsafe, and anyone making you feel unsafe is on my Shit List, far as I'm concerned. I don't care if he's the kids' father or the King of His Own Mind. Yellowtail?"

Good to know where Sid stood on the situation.

"I could use a good yellowtail." Maybe I could cook it over an open bonfire, feel like a real camper, connected to nature and stuff.

Sid sprang into action, happy to be useful, and creaked open his cooler, took out his cleaning knife, and started filleting a fresh catch right there. "I tell you, girl, toxic masculinity is the bane of my existence."

It wasn't easy holding down a chuckle. He was speaking from the heart, and I wouldn't dare interrupt. "Why's that?"

"You think I'm kidding, but it's men like your ex who give us, the good ones, a bad name." He used the sharp edge to scrape away layers upon layers of scales. "But you know, that's how we were raised, men from my generation. Just watch all the movies."

"Which ones?" I asked just to hear Sid talk. There was something comforting about listening to Sid go on, whether or not I was interested in the topic. Just the rhythm of his words soothed me.

"All of them," he said with a flourish of his knife. "Romance movies are the worst. First you have the meet-cute. Usually the woman's put off by something the man does, *but he's just soo hot*, she can't resist him." He mimicked a woman's high-pitched voice. "So, it's okay, right?"

"It's a double standard. I get it."

Sid's eyeballs went big and blue like two oceans. "Ya think? Either that, or the woman says she's not interested. But the man pursues the woman, even though she said she's not interested. Why? Because that son of a bitch won't take no for an answer. Then it becomes a challenge. Everyone thinks he's so damn adorable for trying so hard but really, he's wearing her down."

"You're right. It's all in how they present it." I lifted a handful of sand and let the grains sift between my fingers into a mini pile.

"Last I checked, in the real world…" He wiped the blade against Bruce Springsteen's face. "That's called stalking, and there's nothing meet-cute about it. Finally, the woman gives in, because it's easier letting the dude have his way rather than impressing upon him just how not interested she is, and I'm wondering…what exactly did she fall in love with? His ability to break her spirit? Pfft."

I chuckled even though Sid was right.

"I tell ya, the whole thing gives men the wrong idea. Makes them think women are property, you know? That's why you have this goon—no offense—trying to find you. God forbid he accept that you moved on without him. But nooo, he thinks you're his, he does. Starts calling around the island trying to locate you. Katja," he said pointedly.

"Yes, Sid?"

"Don't you dare mistake that for love." He turned a scolding eye on me that made me feel, for just a minute, like he was my father. "Because it's not. Not even close. It's about power. He can't stand to know that he lost you. This is a game, you see. A dangerous one. And if I were you, I'd be calling the police."

Salty Sid's words pierced my heart, because he wasn't wrong. I'd been giving Nathan the benefit of the doubt when it'd never been about love—only power. His trying to reach me had only ever been about winning. Getting what he wanted.

"I feel wrong calling the police," I said pathetically. "But I know that's wrong. He's the one who left. He's the one trying to find me now."

"It's a fine line, dear," he said. "But I can't tell you what to do. All's I know is that he has no right over you. You don't belong to him."

So much to think about. Nathan was exhibiting predatory behavior. Even if I could be sure he wouldn't do anything drastic, which I couldn't guarantee, I still needed to send the right signals.

"Don't go soft, Katja." Sid jabbed his knife in my direction. I felt each stab in my soul. "Stand your ground. Let him know you won't allow this. Once he sees he's not going to win this one, he should let it go, if he knows what's good for him. And if he doesn't, well…" Sid made a *tsk* sound and shook his head, scraping the last of the scales off the fish, rinsing it in the water. "He'll be sorry."

Watching Sid say that with a knife in his hand gave me chills but also made me feel loved and protected.

"You're right. People bully those who can't or don't stand up for themselves."

"That's right. Ask Lily Autumn. She knows all about it. Anything else for you today, sweetheart? Lobster? Crab? A shotgun under your pillow?"

Though I was laughing on the outside, inside I was crying.

"Got that fine fellow over?" His mood changed, and the twinkle in his eye emerged. Sid could switch gears like a Ferrari.

"Umm…" Should I even try pretending like I didn't know what he was talking about?

"It's okay, nobody told me." He winked. "I just watch everything that happens around here. It's sort of my job to be—"

"A peeping Tom?" I cocked my head.

"To protect! Aww, listen to me, insinuating that you should be cooking for a man. Paradoxical Sid, that's what they should call me."

I threw up my hands. "You know what? I've worked hard. Evan's worked hard. Sure, why not—let's do two lobster tails. How do you cook them?"

"Easy. Just throw them in a pot of boiling water 'til they scream."

"What? That's horrible!" I couldn't cook them that way, not in a million years. "Aren't they dead already?"

"Nope. You want 'em or nah?"

"No, thanks. I'll stick with the yellowtail then. How much do I owe you? I have cash."

"*Pfft*, after all you've been through?" He packed up his cooler and put away his filleting knife. "On me."

"Sid, you can't keep giving me free fish. You have to make a living somehow." I searched my pocket for dollar bills.

"Girly, my houseboat's paid for. I do this for fun. Gives me something to do, people to talk to. Anyhoo, here ya go." He presented me with the fish on butcher paper and tilted the brim of his *Booty Hunter* cap. "See you around!" Hopping back in his boat, he motored on toward Lily's house, whistling a song you might hear in a pirate movie.

"Thank you, Sid! Love you!" I yelled without thinking. How awkward, but true. I'd never felt so loved and cared for as I had here in Skeleton Key.

"Love you back, kiddo!" he called to my relief.

Inside the house, I put the fish inside my temporary cooler filled with all sorts of goodies from Heloise and Jeanine's and my sketches on a pile of wood flooring. "Want yellowtail?" I asked Evan, who was walking by carrying a ladder.

"Where you going to cook it?" he asked. "Portable barbecue?"

"Do you have one?"

"I do. I can bring it later when I bring you the new back lock. Just arrived. Unless, you don't want…"

"No, I do. You can come over." Like Sid said, I couldn't stay in limbo. I had to send the signal that I wouldn't take any more shit. Besides that, I could really use Evan's company.

His smile reminded me of places I'd loved but never been. "Sweet. I'll bring the accoutrements."

"Oo, fancy word." I glanced at my sketches and switched gears like Sid. "Hey, about the theater, Sid says it burned down in an electrical fire following a storm. Do you know anything about that?"

"That's what the only records show, but you know how good century-old documents are. Why?"

I hadn't divulged anything about my dreams or the experiences in the house to him yet, afraid I'd sound insane. "I think it might've been something else."

He put the ladder on its end and grabbed onto it for support. "Like what?"

"Well…this is just based on a hunch I have," I said.

He had on a great listening face. "Go on…"
Tell him. He's your friend.

161

"I've had dreams," I sighed. "In them, it's the 1920s. I'm a little girl looking into the audience of the theater, the same one that used to be here. From above, like secretly. I feel like it's my mom onstage. There's two men—the whole audience is white men—in the back row, whispering. Not watching the show."

"Who are they?" Evan asked. Not who did I *think* they were.

"Not sure. But when they see me, they get angry. They don't *say* they're angry, but I can feel it in my dream. It's like they want to bring my mother down, like maybe she rejected them at one point."

Evan nodded.

"Then, I smell burning. I know this sounds strange. I'm sorry." Rattled by my own honesty, I wring my hands, looking for a way out of the can of worms I opened.

Evan scratched his head. "So, two men plot to destroy a Black woman's booming business in the 1920s by setting it on fire for having rejected their unwanted sexual advances. Sounds legit to me."

"It sounds crazy, I know."

"I said it sounds legit, Kat. Maybe your dreams are the missing link this island's historical society has never found. Maybe this house has needed the right medium living in it all these years."

Medium. I wasn't a medium, but I could see how multiple families over generations didn't last long in the Berry House if Callie and Josephine did want the right medium to convey their story.

"Dreams are useless without evidence." I shrugged.

"Maybe there will be one day. We'll talk about it more later? I gotta…" He pointed to the workers drilling screws into new drywall.

"Of course." I smiled and let him go.

I took my sketches and sat on the front porch bench, looking out at Nanette's house and the rest of Coconut Court. Compared to Lily's street, ours was quieter, but maybe that would change when Lily opened the new bed-and-breakfast.

To my right, a flicker of green caught my attention, and a moment later, an iguana carefully stalked across the windowsill toward me, stopping behind me to look over my shoulder. I made no move. No squeals, no scream.

And though I had no way of proving this, I felt like Iggy was maybe just Callie in physical form. Chillin', studying my sketches, enjoying the sun's warmth, the freedom from the attic. And if someone, a lonely little girl from the past, needed to hang with a friend on the porch who wasn't afraid of her? Well, that was just fine with me.

18

Grilled yellowtail was flaky, lemony, and delicious when made on the BBQ, but it was possible it only seemed that way because Evan made it. He'd brought over his camping grill, a pot I used to make risotto, and a bottle of chardonnay. We dined on the back porch, facing the Atlantic, laughing over the way seagulls fought over scraps. Evan dubbed funny Abbott & Costello-like voices over them, and I nearly snorted risotto out my nose.

How quickly life had changed. One minute, I was working in a drugstore in the middle of nowhere without friends, a husband, or family of my own. I'd quietly accepted my mediocre fate. The next, I was here, watching waves catch fuchsia reflections of the sunset with my male-carpenter-magazine-model hot friend. It was difficult not pausing to reflect on it too much.

Enjoy the moment, Nana said.

We swiveled on the sand when Evan started talking about remodeling plans, facing the house, hopeful gulls surrounding us. He pulled out his phone to look at the saved, old theater blueprints. The real ones were inside, carefully rolled up inside of a cardboard tube he'd bought to protect them. "See this?" He pointed out the rear view of the house, same elevation we were looking at now, except the space between the house and the corner lot was a small, but three-story Victorian-style attachment.

"That was her theater. And this…" He pointed out three lines that disappeared into the margins of the plans with tiny arrows pointing off toward the north. "I think that was a sidewalk of some kind."

"On the beach?"

"A sidewalk, or a boardwalk, or some sort of pathway."

"To where? Or was the plan to continue building one day, but they never got around to it?"

He tapped the phone screen to the next view. "Maybe it led to Annie Jackson's distillery. I can see patrons stopping by for a bottle or two before the show. Were there drunk men in your dreams?"

"Full of them," I replied. "Annie Jackson was Prohibition era, though. 1930s, I think, whereas Josephine's was a whole decade before." Although I thought I remembered the men telling me it was 1928. Could the records be wrong?

"Like I said, maybe the plans were set out to connect the businesses along the beach one day. Wouldn't that have been cool? A beach resort but for illicit activity?" He snorted.

"Not that far-fetched," I said. "Aren't there resorts in the Caribbean now marketed that way? 'Come lay on the sand, get naked, drink your troubles away?' That sort of thing?"

"Yep. And I think it would be amazing to restore, not just this house, but all the other ones on the beach. I've studied them all. The ones on the sand facing the ocean have the most wear which makes sense, since they get blasted with the sun, wind, *and* salt."

I leaned back, sipped from my fancy-schmancy chardonnay. Evan had a determined look in his brow. "You want to build a house from scratch someday?"

My words seemed to give him pause. Then, he nodded. "Kat, I've been drawing houses since I was a kid. I was obsessed. Made my mom buy me every architectural book and magazine I could get my hands on."

"You should've been an architect," I said.

"Being an architect is cool, but I like getting my hands dirty. Doing the work. Making the thing come to life, you know?" When he looked at me, his brown eyes had a fire from within. "There's nothing I love more than before-and-after pics of houses. Old and decrepit on the left, beautiful restoration on the right. I would enjoy building from scratch, but I think I love restoration more. Just haven't gotten that one dream project yet, you know?"

"Why do you think that is?"

He rubbed his thumb and forefinger together, the universal sign for currency. "Money. I go where the immediate jobs are. A bathroom here, a room there, a kitchen here. Never gotten a whole house reno as a commission. What about you?"

"I could never renovate a whole house. I can't even hammer a nail into a piece of wood."

He snorted. "I mean dreams. Don't you have any?"

"Oh, sure."

"Well, let's hear some."

I stared at the house, its three stories, sagging back porch full of potential. "That's not entirely true. I was trying on a new skin again," I said. "I don't really have dreams, Evan. I just wanted to say I did—to see how it feels. Feels good, actually."

"Not a single dream?"

"As a kid, I wanted to have big boobs like Elvira, Mistress of the Dark. Does that count?"

He let his eyes go wide for a second before shaking his head. "You're kidding, right? I mean, I love me some Elvira, but…"

"Dead serious. A teen boy down my street where my grandmother lived used to keep his garage open while he tinkered on his car, and every day I used to ride my bike past his house and see his poster of Elvira on the garage wall. She was lying on her side like a slinky cat, boobs pushed together, all sexy and full of confidence. I loved that confidence. I wanted that confidence so badly."

That sounded so pathetic next to Evan's dream of renovating beautiful homes, but it was true. I had no aspirations as a kid. I'd watched so many princess movies, I only wanted to marry and have kids.

"Other than marrying someone who would take care of me, no, I didn't have any dreams," I said. "Evan, I grew up thinking my lot in life was to marry, be a mom, a wife, and that's it. Host parties, put Christmas gifts under the tree…nothing more. I've always admired women with careers, but I never had that kind of drive."

"Why do you think that is?" he asked.

"I wasn't that smart in school."

"But you're smart out of school," he said.

"Thanks, but I always assumed careers were for women stronger and smarter than I was. Women with balls."

"Women with balls," Evan repeated, leaning back. "Basically, you just described yourself."

I gave him an appreciative smile. "Now that I'm forty-four, I know I could've had a career of some kind, but at this point…"

"Nah, nah, nah," he cut me off. "Don't you say it's too late. You're not even halfway through your life."

"At best, I'm halfway, yes."

"Fine. But it's still not too late. You know what my mother did at your age?" He waited for me to guess.

"Joined the circus?"

"You're not wrong. She went back to college, got her degree in education, and became a junior high school math teacher."

"That's freakin' amazing."

"Exactly. She was so proud, and we were all proud for her. The school had all these teachers who were tired of the job by her age, whereas she was excited to teach. And so she ended up becoming every kid's favorite teacher. You know how hard it is to become anyone's favorite *math* teacher?"

I giggled. "The moral of the story is that I can do it."

"Not only can you do it, but you should. Because what else are you going to do? You have half a life left, girl."

"I always assumed I'd become a grandma."

A sigh from Evan. It must've been frustrating for him to try and help me, only to have me backhand his every serve. But the truth was—I needed to believe in myself more than I needed him, or anybody, to believe in me.

I knew that.

I just needed to start feeling it.

"Being a grandmother would be fun. But there has to be more. What happens when you don't see your grandkids all the time? What do you do in your own time?" Evan swiveled his butt in the sand to face me and, in a surprise but wholly welcome move, took my hands. "Kat, your girls are in college, right? Now's the perfect time to start new. Something for yourself. You have nowhere to go but up." He shook my hands like he wanted to shake sense into me.

I squeezed his hands, his last words lingering on my mind. "You're good at pep-talking."

"I'm good at other things, too." His eyebrows flared. Eyes took on a naughtier stare that made my stomach flip, sending fire through my loins.

I sighed. "I know what I need to do, Evan. Thank you for reminding me. It's just…" I shook my head. What was my problem?

"You need closure." Words I'd internally understood deep down but hadn't been able to vocalize.

I looked at him.

"Maybe it's time to close the door. On the last chapter of your life. Do it. Make it official. Declare it's time to move on. For five weeks, I've watched you hang on, talk about the past, about your ex, about the life you used to live. One foot in this world, one foot in your past."

Damn.

"It's not my place, Kat. I'm sorry if I'm out of line here, but we're friends. I want to see you succeed. When I look at you, I see someone figuring out who she is, but I also see someone with huge potential. You're funny, hardworking, and smart as heck. You have to see it for yourself."

Tearing my gaze away from him, I glanced at the house under renovation again. I was the Berry House, undergoing change. I was the Berry House covered in scaffolding, ladders, and loose screws everywhere. Once ready, however, the work put into it would turn out beautiful. And worth the trouble.

It was no surprise that we ended up drinking the whole bottle of chardonnay. Or that we ended up in each other's arms, restlessly, urgently needing more than kissing, or that I straddled him on the beach with our clothes on, desperately trying to put out the fire in my body, knowing it would require more, kissing until kissing would no longer quench it.

Or that we tumbled up the stairs and fell into my bed, despite my fearful self telling me to wait—until the last chapter had closed. Realizing it didn't need to close cleanly. There could be overlap, one chapter slowly diffusing into the other, like scenes did in movies all the time.

All was well. No need to feel guilt.

Nor was it a surprise when he slept over again. Or that he was still asleep by the time I heard the first work trucks arrive outside the house. Because, ahem—I'd worked him hard. Yes, I had, indeedly-dee, and for those first few moments of the day, before the crew came in and started hammering, buzzsawing, and making a hell of a noise, I watched, mesmerized, as Evan slept, his bare, wide chest rose and fell with even breath, one naked arm tucked underneath his head. Were men's underarms sexy? Evan made them sexy.

Quietly, I curled up to him. His arm folded over me, keeping me safe. He murmured something about needing to get up.

Close the door on the last chapter.

I had to do something to put it all behind me. Only then would I be able to move forward. Only then I might be able to put Katja, the mother and wife, aside and start a new identity of my own. I could still be a mother, of course, but there was a well of potential inside of me. I had too much to give—to others, but also to myself.

All this was fresh on my mind when I heard the workers knock, impatient for Evan to let them in, so while he used the bathroom to get ready, I threw on clothes and groggily headed downstairs to open the door—

—and found Nathan standing there.

19

I gasped, gripped the door.

His jawline was firm. Eyes glassy. Raving. "How the hell are you affording to stay in *this* house?"

That was his first question? Not "How are you?" or "Where have you been?"

"I…" Felt lightheaded, my stomach weak, my tone of voice meek and cautious. "I work here."

"You work here?" The vein in his temple pulsated. "How the hell do you work here? Why haven't you been answering any of my calls or texts, Kitty Kat?"

Kitty Kat—a name he used so long ago now sounded out of place and context. I hated it. "I got a job on a TV show, Nathan."

"On a TV show." He burst out a quick laugh.

"Not on a TV show. As an assistant. It's a long story. You weren't around," I added, just to make my point.

"You don't need to clarify, Kitty Kat. I know you could never be on a TV show." More laughing. I was hilarious to him, and just like that, I felt like shit again.

From their cars and trucks, workers looked on with caution. Nathan took a few slow steps toward me, but I instinctively closed the door a bit, which made him even angrier. His hand shot out to hold it back. "I wasn't around because I made a mistake, Katja. I made a mistake, and when men make mistakes, they come back home. To their wives. That's what a *man* does—acknowledges when he's wrong."

The masked woman in my bed probably dumped his ass when she realized what a loser he was, and that was why he was back. He had nowhere else to go. He didn't give a shit about me or anybody. One way or another, I had to make him understand it was over, like everyone on this island had told me.

"I think you should go," I stammered, pushing the door shut again, but he pushed back harder, propping it open. "Nathan, this isn't my house. We can't argue here. We'll go somewhere…we'll talk."

He spoke through clenched teeth. "Like you have to tell me this ain't your house. Of course, it ain't your house, Kitty Kat. You could never afford a place like this. What are you, cleaning for them? You're a cleaning lady?" His wise-cracking smile made me want to punch him in the tobacco-stained teeth.

Like I could never be more, like I was destined to clean up after other people—people more successful than me. But he wasn't wrong, so what right did I have to be mad? It was true. But it was only true because of him.

"Whose fault is that?" I shook from head to toe with rage. "You're the one who didn't want me going to school. Women don't need a degree. Women don't need jobs. Women need to stay home, take care of children. Isn't that what you said, Nathan?"

"I did," he said. "Because it's true. You know what happens when women forget their place? This." He gestured to the house and surroundings, as if there were anything offensive about it. "This is what happens. She starts getting brave—oh, so independent—then before you know it, she's gone, and I have to go on a wild fucking goose chase across the country just to find my own wife."

"Not your wife…" I whispered, tears threatening to sprout. I pushed them back. I wouldn't let him see me crying. He didn't deserve it.

Don't let him scare you, Nana's voice coached from the sidelines. I might've shaken my head to dislodge it. As much as I loved my grandmother, she wasn't helping, and there wasn't a damned thing she could've said that I didn't already know.

"I'm not your wife anymore," I said.

"What's that?"

"You heard me. I stopped being your wife the moment you left. I thought I made that clear with the divorce paperwork you were given, the ones you never signed. The one keeping us in a holding pattern is you, Nathan. I'm ready to move on. Whether or not you are, too, you need to go now."

Behind me, I heard boots stomping down the stairs. My heart stopped. I was not ready for a showdown. Nathan's steel gray eyes narrowed, as he peered over my shoulder. "Someone with you?"

Evan stepped up behind me. "Everything okay out here?"

"He's…a worker," I said to Nathan, as if he had any right to an explanation. "A friend," I corrected. Evan did not deserve to be reduced to someone as trivial as a "worker" and I was done caring if Nathan got mad. He was surrounded by burly men with power tools. What was he going to do—hurt me?

"Works on the house, or on you?" Nathan gave a fake snort. "Hey, bud. I'm her husband." He reached out with a handshake and a salty grin, but Evan wouldn't take it.

"I believe Katja told you to go," Evan said, as other men began crowding the front porch.

"And I believe it better if you stayed out of our *businessss*," Nathan hissed. He fixed his stare on me again. "It's time to go home, Kitty Kat. The girls need you." He reached for my arm, which spurred Evan to jump forward, but I could handle it.

I yanked my arm back. It might've been the overabundance of men willing to rearrange Nathan's facial features, but I felt more emboldened than ever. "The girls don't need me. That's because I did an amazing job preparing them for life. They know I'm here. They're proud of me, unlike you. Now, get out."

A look of confusion swept over Nathan's face. I knew it was because the girls had insisted they didn't know where I'd gone when he'd asked. They'd lied to protect me, just like I knew they would.

"I drove down all this way, and I'm not leaving without my wife. I don't care what papers you sent—in God's eyes, you will always be mine."

"Buddy, you couldn't be more wrong." Evan pushed past me onto the front porch, as Nathan took a couple of steps back. Neither was a particularly tall man, but Evan was younger, stronger, more menacing in bulk and stature next to Nathan's slight, out-of-shape frame. "How many times does she have to say it? Get the hell out before we call authorities. Leave nicely and there won't be any trouble. That's how it works. You have two seconds to decide."

One of Evan's workers had come to stand behind Nathan. "That's generous of you. I wouldn't even give him one. Let's go—you're done here." The man clapped a hand onto Nathan's shoulder and forced him to turn.

Nathan relented as his gaze burned a hole into my brain. "I'll be back then we're going home."

"You and what army? Get the fuck out, friend," Evan spat, pointing toward the street until Nathan had reached the sidewalk, at which point Evan's worker let him go with a shove. For the splittest of seconds, I felt sorry for Nathan. He seemed smaller than I remembered him, weaker, a sadder excuse of a man, and I hated— hated—that I'd ever seen anything in him. But that was because I'd never seen much in myself to begin with.

That ended now.

"What do you mean he showed up?"

Lily dragged me to the guest living room, away from the kitchen where I'd spilled the details about this morning's event. The two employees cleaning up after brunch and the guests in the dining room going over Keys recreation options were all within earshot.

I was in tears. "I thought it was one of the construction workers at my door, so I went down to answer it. I didn't think it'd be Nathan. I don't know how he found the exact house."

"Excuse me, Ms. Autumn?" One of the women from the kitchen slipped out and sidled up. "I'm sorry. I overheard you. You said a man came to the house looking for you?" She looked at me.

"Yes," both Lily and I replied.

"I was at the dollar store last night. There was a man after me paying for a bag of candy and a Sprite. The cashier began ringing him up. He asked if she'd seen his wife then showed a photo on his phone. I thought it was strange, like the kind of thing private investigators do in movies."

I swiped my forehead. "Candy and Sprite. That has Nathan written all over it."

She wiped her hand on a towel. "I have no idea what the cashier told him. I was out the door. But now that I hear you talking about it, I'm thinking that was probably him. I'm sorry. If I'd known, I would've intervened."

"It's okay, Celia," Lily said. "Thank you for telling us."

"Yes, it's okay. Thank you," I said, too. At some point, I had to take responsibility for my own shitstorm. It wasn't anybody's fault Nathan had found me but my own.

Lily waited for Celia to return to the kitchen, then she turned to me. "Do we need to call the police?"

I wasn't sure. Part of me, the stupid part that was learning the hard way, knew Nathan was more bark than bite. In all the years we'd been together, he'd never physically hurt me. He didn't have to. I gave in too easily. But now?

"He said he would come back, but…"

"Was Evan there?"

I swallowed. "Yes. He…he stayed with me last night."

Lily gave me a sly look that melted into a smile.

"What?" I laughed.

"Nice job, friend. Keep him around until we know for sure your ex won't be back."

"Okay. I'm sorry if that's not in the rules, Ms. Lily. It was after hours, and he's been such a good friend to me."

"No…" She held up a finger. "What you do on your own time is none of my business. Besides, I know all too well how having a new male presence can help dislodge the old one. You know what else will help?"

"Tequila?"

She looked to the kitchen to make sure no one could hear her then raised one eyebrow. "Do you have anything of your ex's? A shirt maybe? Something that belonged to him?"

"I didn't bring much with me. Certainly not his clothes."

"Nothing that would have his energy?"

I didn't know where she was going with this, but being who she was, I had a vague idea. "I might have something. I don't want to admit it, though."

"Katja, if we're going to get you on the right path once and for all, you're going to have to trust me."

"I have a blanket."

"A blanket."

"Yes. With SpongeBob on it. I know it sounds stupid, but it's the one I found him having sex on with that woman."

178

"So, you took possession of it," Lily said with complete understanding.

I nodded, tears stinging my eyes.

"Shh, it's okay to do that. We hold onto things as a way of reclaiming what others took from us. Our pride, sense of safety, even our dignity. You have it with you?"

I nodded. "It's at the house."

Lily smiled gently, like a sister or a best friend might. "Bring it tonight. There's a full moon at midnight, and I think it's time for another moon party."

"Okay. Thank you, Lily." I felt better knowing she wasn't upset with me in any way. "I'll see you tonight." I started to go.

"Oh, Katja?"

"Yes?" I whirled around, refreshed.

"Do you still have all those dolls you found while cleaning, or did you give them away?"

My heart skipped a beat. "I…still have them."

"Whew. Okay. The previous owners called, asking if they could have them back. After they left, they felt they should've taken the dolls with them."

My head felt light. Sam and I had already transformed about ten of them. "Did they say why?"

She gave a shrug. "Said they might be valuable. And since they sold the property to me at such a great price, I told them I'd check and see. You didn't want them, did you?"

20

Shit. Shit, shit.

Double shit. Triple shit.

Instead of answering her question straight, I'd offered a vague, "Let me see where they're at. I'll get back to you."

Now, trudging back to the house, trying not to hyperventilate, I mentally reviewed all Lily had told me when I first arrived: the previous owners had left stuff behind; they'd left in a hurry; I was asked to separate anything that might be of interest to Lily in case she opened another *Dead & Breakfast*. I could keep whatever else I wanted or donate. I'd kept the dolls, painted over many of them, and now she was telling me they might be valuable??

Shit.

Was I in trouble? I shouldn't be.

She might be disappointed that the dolls were no longer in their original state, and that she might not be able to return them, but I hadn't done anything wrong, I kept telling myself. The worst part was that my surprise for her might be altogether foiled. Scratch that—the worst part was that I might've ruined valuable dolls that technically belonged to her!

I hurried up the steps of my house—of her house. I didn't have a house, because only Nathan's name was on our deed. Rushing inside, paranoid that I'd run into Nathan again, I stormed up the stairs, ignoring the crew ripping out old paneling in the dining room. Inside my bedroom, I closed the door and sat on the bed, breathing in and out slowly.

Shit was hitting the fan.

I could only tackle one problem at a time, however. I decided to deal with the easiest one first. Lily asked me to find an item of Nathan's that would carry his energy for something she planned to do. I had my suspicions. I opened the nightstand drawer and fished out the infamous SpongeBob blanket. I hadn't used it at all since that day, so it still had Nathan-ness all over it.

Rushing out, I headed back downstairs when I spotted Sam poking his head up the stairwell, front door wide open behind him. "Hi." He waved. "Are you okay? I heard some stuff went on this morning."

"I'm fine, I think." I scuttled downstairs.

"If you need help, or you need somebody to watch over you, I'm available."

My heart transmuted to liquid form and bled all over the stairwell. "That's incredibly sweet of you, Sam. I've got several pairs of eyes keeping out for me, but I wouldn't mind another set. Text me if you see him driving around the neighborhood."

"Are you going to call the cops on him? Get a restraining order?"

"I will if I see him again," I promised. "I'm done getting harassed. He thinks I'm the same woman he last saw, but he won't know what hit him if he comes back."

Sam was handsome when he smiled. "That's what I like to hear. Fuck bullies."

"Yeah," I agreed. "Oh! Actually, I do need your help with something."

His eyes lit up. He nodded in earnest. "Yeah, sure. Anything."

"Find the ugliest, newest of the dolls I've left at your house. Any of the ones unpainted yet. Do we have any?"

"We have the ones in that box labeled DONATE."

"Perfect. Get one from there, and here…" I pulled out my phone, thumbed through my camera roll for a photo of Nathan, and texted it to Sam. "See this pic of my ex? Go ahead and give the doll a new face. Make it look as much like him as possible."

Sam glanced at his own phone and bristled. "Ew, that's him? He's not ugly, but he looks rude as hell."

"He is. Very rude. And the more of his personality you can get into his face, the better."

"Am I thinking what you're thinking?" Sam asked.

"If you're half as witchy as you say you are, yes." I lifted the SpongeBob blanket. "And this, I have a feeling, will go on the doll, too."

"You're making a voodoo doll of your ex." Sam's eyes split into a hundred different colors. I'd never seen him come so alive. "That's so fucking cool."

"I never said that." I cupped his chin maternally. "Speak none of this to your grandmother. Last thing I need is Nanette thinking I've corrupted her grandson."

He zipped his mouth and mimicked throwing away the key. "Mffhsdmadsl."

"Exactly."

Once the moon had risen, and the workers had all gone home (except for Evan who insisted on hanging back in case of Return of the Nathan), Sam and I headed out to the beach. Earlier, I'd asked Lily if I could bring a guest to her moon party.

Depends, she'd said. *Who?* When I'd replied Sam, because Sam was quite witchy, Ms. Lily had been sweet enough to reply with YES and a bunch of exclamation points.

Inside the bag I carried were the SpongeBob blanket, a naked baby doll with the repainted face of Nathan on it (Sam and I broke into fits of giggles when he'd shown it to me), and a bottle of red wine I'd asked Evan to please pick up for me to share with the ladies. Never come to a party empty-handed.

Already, the ladies were on the beach, starting another bonfire. From a distance, they looked like legit witches, cackling and laughing with reckless abandon. Lily sat on the sand, kicking up her bare feet, while Heloise danced to a Stevie Nicks song pouring from a speaker, and Jeanine stared at the ocean in deep thought.

"I've always wondered what they were doing," Sam said giddily, like a rock groupie invited to a backstage party. "I'd watch them from the beach and wonder what it would take to be included."

"Aww, I felt the same the first time I saw them."

"How did you get in?" he asked.

"I just walked up to them and started talking."

"Iconic," Sam muttered. "And you're sure it's okay that I come along?"

"Yes." I hooked my arm through his. "Lily was quite happy to hear it."

Sam slowly breathed through his nose. "Cool."

We passed Heloise's grandmother's glass ball, past the row of tall sea grass, onto Lily's stretch of the beach. "Hello, ladies."

Three already-buzzed women whipped their heads our way. "Helloooo!" Lily shot to her feet in a second, stumbling over a small dune then wiping her butt free of debris. "Welcome, welcome!" She opened her arms to me and Sam.

"Thank you for having me," Sam said, surprised, it seemed, by Lily's mini hug and Heloise's kiss on the cheek.

"Of course. Our pleasure. We've been meaning to introduce ourselves to you," Lily said, "but Nanette always said you were sleeping."

If that was true, that made me sad. Was Nanette trying to keep her trans grandson a secret from the neighborhood?

"I do sleep sort of late," Sam replied. "Plus, I never wanted to bother you, 'cause I mean, you're Lily Fucking Autumn. I'm super happy to be meeting you. I've watched every episode of your show."

"Aww, thank you! That means so much to me." Lily patted Sam on the back and smiled at me as a silent thanks for bringing him. "Did you hear that? I'm Lily

'Fucking' Autumn. May just have to change the intro for Season 2."

Jeanine skulked over with her wine glass in the air. "And the coven grows!" she cried, taking my hand and twirling herself underneath my arm. Sam and I laughed at her shenanigans. Jeanine was so Jeanine.

Coven. I never thought of these women as a coven before. Or, rather, as me being a part of a coven, but if by coven, she meant women—people, regardless of gender—who got together to make shit happen for themselves, then I was now happily part of a coven.

"My ex will lose his mind when he hears this," I said.

Holy shit, Nana, I'm in a coven.

All I heard was Nana's cackle in my head.

"Oh, we won't tell him, now, will we?" Heloise came over with a tray of little bites that looked like prosciutto with cheese. "Take. Eat. Food."

The hospitality was off the charts, but I supposed that three women who ran a bed-and-breakfast would know a thing or two about hostessing. Still, something told me they saved the best for themselves, and I was honored to be a part of it.

"Did you bring…the thing?" Lily wiggled her eyebrows.

"Yes." I reached into the bag and pulled out the SpongeBob blanket. "Here. And not only did I bring the thing, I brought another thing. Don't laugh, okay?"

"Can't promise anything," Lily said. Heloise and Jeanine gathered around.

I produced the doll inside the bag—the naked baby doll with a mean-spirited male face painted on. Sam and I had worked all afternoon to get his hair cut and re-styled in the same short side-part as my ex.

"What in the hairballs?" Heloise doubled over and tripped in the sand. "What is this…" Long, red-painted fingernails curled around the doll, as she doubled over again in laughter.

"That is the most disgusting thing I've ever seen!" Lily cried, also clutching the doll, wiping her eyes of tears.

Sam and I glanced at each other, beaming at the reaction. "I told you," I said to Sam.

"This is an anatomically correct representation of your ex-husband, yes?" Jeanine pressed a forefinger into the doll's flat, naked, genderless crotch, feeling out the soft filling of the main body.

After we'd all had a good laugh, I took the doll, placed it on the picnic table, and draped the microfiber blanket over him. "I think he'll look good in yellow and Bikini Bottom flowers. What do you all think?"

"Girl, this is too much." Heloise had to sit down and take a sip of her wine. "I swear, these moon parties get more and more crazy every time, Lily."

"Yeah, Pulitzer, I suspect that soon, we'll be making flying ointment and riding around on real brooms. Real ointment, not the metaphorical ointment that represents…you know…"

"I'm lost," I said.

Sam leaned into my ear. "She's talking about in the old days, when witches made flying ointment, it was code for lube. Riding a broomstick was code for masturbation. So, riding on a broomstick meant taking care of business by yourself without a man."

"What?" I spat. "How do you know these things? You're too young to know stuff like that."

"Hey." Sam flipped his palms up. "I know my witch history."

"You sure do," Heloise agreed. "Now, shall we get started? It'll be a full moon in exactly forty-three minutes, ladies—excuse me, ladies and gentlemen—and we have much to do to get ready."

Sam's proud smile at being acknowledged as a gentleman warmed my heart. Seeing him come out of his shell made me so happy, even if nothing else came out of being here tonight, at least I got to see that.

Lily took a stack of long sticks from the picnic table and passed them out. "Tonight, we'll use a visualization technique that I used last year before my life changed forever. I want you all to find a spot in the sand and draw a picture."

"Can it be stick figures?" Jeanine asked.

"Doesn't matter how much of an artist you are. All that matters is the intention you put into it. Now, Katja, we talked earlier. You know what you need to visualize."

"Letting go of Nathan. Being on my own…"

"Yes, in fact, you're not even going to use his name anymore tonight. Names give power, and the less you use it, the less power he'll have over you. You want to almost forget who he is."

I nodded, but something about that felt wrong. After all, Nathan (what's-his-name) had slept in the same bed with me for over twenty-two years, and given me two, beautiful daughters, but I understood. For the purposes of moving on, I had to imagine him way back in my rearview mirror.

"It's just a psychological tool," Heloise explained, as if she understood my worry. "We know he was a major part of your life, love. Nobody is asking you to forget your past. Think of it as starting a new chapter. Trust me, I've been where you are."

I did trust her, implicitly. All these women.

And all the men of this island, too.

In seven weeks, I'd earned a family, and because of that, I put my life in their collective hands. Starting now, here on this beach, with these beautiful people, I was beginning a new chapter, and I'd never been more grateful.

21

On a full moon in the warm August breeze, I drew like I've never drawn before. As music filled the air, I drew a house that looked like the Berry House, though honestly, I would take any house. I drew the ocean behind it, because I'd grown to love the ocean so much since I'd been here. I couldn't imagine not living next to it now. Then, I added myself next to the house wearing a big smile, because this was a new start to life, and I wanted to do more smiling from now on.

I leaned back to see how it was going so far.

Pretty good.

I added two girls—women, I should say—beside me. My daughters, Hailey and Remy. I knew they would likely go on to start their own lives after graduation, but drawing them in meant I wanted to keep them as a major part of my life.

On my other side, I drew a little girl—Callie. Why was I drawing her? I didn't know. Regardless of where I lived after this, I hoped to keep in touch with her. Like Sam, she needed someone to hang out with, to play with, and I would be up for tea parties with dolls any day!

Next to her, I drew an iguana. Fine, maybe I was drawing my current life instead of a future one, but other than my ex harassing me, things were starting to turn around, and Iggy, Callie, or whoever the ghost lizard was, had been a part of that. My drawing looked pretty good. Everyone else was quietly drawing too, in their own worlds. I caught glimpses of boats, houses, stars, cats, and stick figures holding hands with other stick figures.

Studying mine, I wondered if I should add Evan to my drawing. He'd been a lovely part of my time here, too, but was he in my future? Did I want to start a new relationship? I wasn't sure. It was way too early. Maybe a future chapter and full moon would uncover that, but for now, I decided to leave him out of my drawing. Instead, I wrote "Thank you" inside a heart next to the house. That was a secret message for me to be grateful for how much he'd helped me so far. I didn't have to know everything right now.

"I like what you've done," Jeanine sidled up to my drawing like an art teacher. I waited for her wisecracks, but she had none. "Dream big, Katja," was all she said. "Dream big." She walked away.

Yes.

That had been a huge problem in my past, not dreaming big enough, assuming that a man would take care of all my needs, not listening to Nana when I was young and first meeting "what's his name." She'd tried telling me to keep looking, that he wasn't the only fish in the sea, that I should make something of myself first. But I hadn't listened. As a result, her voice had haunted me ever since. But what if it wasn't Nana? What if Nana's voice all this time had been my own, telling me what to do? Maybe if I'd spent more time working on my goals, cultivated a career, I wouldn't be starting from scratch like I was now.

"Better late than never," I murmured.

"Hear, hear," I heard Lily say from ten feet away, as she put the final touches on her own drawing.

Sam was working diligently on his sketch way over there. Looked like a stage and movie camera, seats, and a bucket of popcorn. I smiled, "You'll make it there," I said to him. He looked at me and beamed. I had no doubt that kid would go places. He was full of talent. He just had to step out of the dark, into the light, where others could appreciate him as much as I did.

I added Sam to my drawing, too. Yes, I already had two kids of my own, but I had more love to give children who needed me, especially if Sam's mama wasn't too keen on his choices. Well, I'd be. Everyone needed to feel loved and included in this world.

After all our drawings were done, Heloise had us all hold hands. "Goddess moon," she recited, "hold our drawings under your light, help our dreams come true soon." She asked us to repeat her chant.

"Goddess moon, hold our drawings under your light, and help our dreams come true soon," we said in unison.

Already, the good vibes were flowing. Already, I felt positive changes in the air. Whether that was real magic or a psychological shift that would help create my own magic didn't matter. Did it? If the result was the same?

Lily called us over to the picnic table, which we cleared of food and dishes to lay out the ugly-ass doll of what's-his-name, along with sewing scissors, thread, needle, more face paints in case we needed them, the SpongeBob blanket, and more. As we all stood around itching to get our hands on the materials, Lily said, "Let's get to work, witches!" and

Something about that made me feel powerful. So much a part of a team. I'd never been part of a team before, even when I'd volunteered for Girl Scouts parent. This was different—this was to enact change.

We marked the SpongeBob blanket in the shape of the doll and cut out the pieces. Then we made a little pair of pants, a little shirt, shoes, and a belt all out of the material that my ex had used night after night to sit on the couch watching television, a habit I'd learned from him. As much as I loved *Witch of Key Lime Lane*, I'd be using more of my time to create new hobbies and interests from now on. Who knew how many of those nights my ex had plotted his disloyalty? If energy really did stick to physical objects, then this blanket reeked of his betrayal, and I was happy to get rid of it.

Once the doll was fitted with N's clothes, Lily told me to take it and follow her to the fire. We all walked solemnly, like we were at a funeral procession. We stood around the blaze at five different points. Not gonna lie—we looked like real witches, the kind that stripped down naked and danced under the moonlight, holding hands, while chanting about air, fire, water, and earth, and I realized it was time to stop acting surprised by that. Because here was the truth—we *were* those kinds of witches, and I was one of them now.

While Heloise and Jeanine recited words about the goddess moon, the universe, the winds of the east

carrying my pain out to the waters of the west for them
to take them away, I swayed in the crackling heat, relaxed
from the wine and positive energy swirling around.

"You'll need to say the next words yourself, Kat,"
Lily said. "Tell the fire everything you wish to burn
away."

"Fat. Calories. Twenty pounds," I said, because
comedy eased tension, and I was feeling it.

The ladies and Sam chuckled then quickly
resumed their serious demeanors. "Tell the universe you
wish to bind your ex from causing you further harm,"
Lily said. "Go ahead. We'll help you if you need it."

I studied them all standing guard, helping
someone like me, someone who'd waited too long to help
herself. They stood protecting a sacred circle of
friendship and self-reliance while I made peace with my
life. It felt strange praying to God, the universe, the
elements, or whoever with them standing around, but I
closed my eyes and pretended I was alone.

My sigh was the heaviest object on the beach. I
felt it travel around me then burn away in the fire.
"God," I said. "I would like for my ex-husband to leave
me alone."

"Say it like it's happening now. Use present tense
verbs," Jeanine added. "I bind my ex-husband…"

I nodded and tried again.

"I bind my ex-husband from doing me more
harm. He leaves me alone to live a new life. We go our
separate ways," I said, as tears rose into my eyes. A lone
sob, out of nowhere, escaped my throat. One by one, my
friends gathered around me, holding my free hand and

shoulders. "Take this effigy of…him…and burn not him, but his memory, releasing me forever."

"Release Katja forever," Heloise said, her eyes closed, the fire reflecting off her shiny eyelids.

"When you're ready, throw him in the fire," Lily said.

"Wait, is this going to hurt him?" I asked, swiping the back of my hand across my eyes.

"No, love," Heloise said. "It's not like the movies when they stick a pin in and it hurts. The truth is more metaphorical, symbolic."

"Got it." I nodded, holding the doll in both hands. I was ready to let him go then. Ready to close that chapter behind me and look forward to a shiny new future. "Burn, motherfucker," I said, tossing the doll into the fire.

For four days, I felt peace unlike I'd never known. That moon party had changed my life forever. I never knew people could come together so wholly, respectfully with good intentions, like the way I always felt Holy Communion should be—one with God and the universe. Not once did I wonder if my ex would return, and I'd found myself referring to him as Nahtan (Nathan, but backwards, going away). Not once did I hesitate whenever there was a knock at the door.

Lily had told me it was very important that I believe in my magic. If I doubted, for even a second, whether it would work, then it wouldn't. Witchcraft was all faith. I imagined that prayer worked the same way in church. The two paths of spirituality weren't all that different from each other, the more I thought about it.

Mostly, I spent the four days cleaning up house, top to bottom. Evan's crew had finished the living room and kitchen, and the house looked brand new from the inside. They'd even come to paint the outside, and hoo! Let me tell you how new a house could look with a fresh coat of paint. Overall, I was so proud of the Berry House, but I felt sad at the same time, because soon, I'd be gone.

I'd done my job and done it well. The network executives would be here in a few days, and that gave Lily time to come by each day for inspection and to brainstorm theme ideas for the 2nd season. It was time to present all my hard work, to bust out my sketches and dolls to show Lily.

When she arrived, the last of the crew was cleaning up, Evan was outside discussing with another worker, and it was as good a time as any. We sat down on a new sofa Lily had bought and temporarily put in the living room with the fresh, gray walls.

"I love gray walls," she sighed. "Feels like a blank slate, doesn't it? Like, even if I end up changing it later, or if all goes well, the network converts the house to a whole other theme and colors, I still love starting with gray walls."

I nodded, in another world of thought. "I want to thank you."

"For what?" She looked at me, hands folded in her lap.

"My gosh. For asking me to be here, for giving me this opportunity, for teaching me magic, how to bind my ex. I mean, what blessing in my life wasn't because of you? Besides, I think it worked."

"Has he come by?"

"Not at all," I said. "I think he left. Anyway, I know you have a meeting later to prepare for, but when I first arrived, you asked me to come up with any ideas I might have for a new *Dead & Breakfast*." I lifted my sketchbook from the floor, along with the architectural plans I'd found in the attic.

"Oh?" Her face lit up when she saw I'd come prepared.

"Yes, Ms. Lily, I, too, can put together a presentation. I have so much to tell you. You've been busy with travel, and I've been having issues, so I was waiting for the right moment. I guess this is it." I let out a sigh and opened my sketchbook. "Keeping in mind that I'm not an interior designer…"

She held up a finger. "No need to start with the negative, Kat. What if you *are* a designer? I mean, if you designed something, doesn't that make you a designer?"

"True." She would never, ever know how much hearing that from her meant to me. I showed her my chicken scratches on paper. "There's so much history here," I said. "A theater that burned down years ago, trunks full of costumes, dolls for miles and miles."

"Speaking of which," she tapped her forehead, "I need to get back to the previous owners about the dolls."

"About that…" My leg shook nervously. "I have the dolls. I'll show a few to you in a second, but I think the new *Dead & Breakfast* should match up with Sylvie & Lily's. Going with a similar theme, I think it would be nice to do another gothic, Victorian style, but line the walls with—"

"Ghosts?"

"Creepy dolls."

"Ohh, I'm listening."

"People love creepy dolls. You can find them all over Etsy. Repurposed, repainted, old dolls given snazzy new lives. Some are insanely amazing, and well...Sam and I have been busy..." I moved from the couch into the kitchen where I'd left a bag of dolls I'd brought over from Nanette's. Plucking one gorgeous baby out, I held it up for Lily to see.

"First of all, I'm so, so sorry I did this. After you told me the previous owners wanted the dolls back, that they might be valuable, I stopped refurbishing them. And just so you know, we didn't touch the oldest ones, the composite dolls from the earlier days, only the newer, plastic ones."

"May I see?" Lily took the doll from my hands, eyes roving, gazing, admiring the handiwork. "Kat, this is absolutely gorgeous. I've seen this done before, but yours rivals the ones I've seen. Easily some of the best work I've seen."

"Sam painted the faces. I redid their clothes. Some of them you'll see have burlesque dresses, garters, feather boas, stockings, little shoes which I made from plaster and resin."

"I am in complete awe..."

"I imagine this whole wall," I said, gesturing to the new wall the men had built, "covered with shelves that hold these dolls. Every guest room could be a different color—red plush and theater velvet, green for the prep and makeup room, purple because purple is badass goth." I pulled out another doll, then another, then another, lining them all up on the couch for Lily to see.

She touched her lips.

"Are you mad?"

"Why would I be?"

"Because I did this. I should've kept them aside, not touched them, in case the owners wanted them back, but you told me they left everything behind. You said I should set aside items I felt you could use, and well…then I got the idea to do this. Even if you didn't like them, I would find a use for them. I'm not one for letting things go to waste. I just never imagined they would ask for them back."

"Screw them," she said.

I almost swallowed my tongue. "Sorry?"

"Screw them. They said we could do whatever we wanted with the items they left, then came around asking for them back? I told them I'd look. If we still had them, sure I'd give them back their dolls, but this is an infinitely way cooler use for them, Kat." She examined my sketches and held up a different doll for minutes at a time, positioning each one in the air where I could practically see ideas racing through her mind.

"I'm so relieved to hear you say that. I thought I was in deep trouble."

"Not at all! I love this so much. You have no idea. This is exactly what I was hoping for when I hired you."

"Really?"

She emanated a sisterly smile. "Yes. One, you're a fan of the show. Two, you're imaginative. And three, you were ready to be a part of something. I knew, once you got here, that creative juices would start flowing."

"So, you're not mad then."

"For goodness sake. NO! I don't anger easily, first of all, Kat, and second, we're more alike than you think! I would've done the same thing. Hell, I would've sold the dolls behind my back just to make a buck. That is, if I was sure they were garbage."

"I almost did that," I admitted with a blush. "There's something else I want to show you. I've been holding onto this for the right moment. You've been so busy." I took out the architectural plans and laid them out on the floor.

"What is this?" She sat cross-legged beside them and gaped open-mouthed at the blueprints.

"I found them in the attic. It's to the old theater. You'll never believe this, but the woman who built this house, Josephine, who owned and operated the theater? She had a little girl."

Lily's interest flashed in her eyes. "I've heard this rumor."

"And I'm not sure why, but since I've been here, my psychic abilities have opened up. She's shown herself to me several times. She comes into my dreams. She even took me to the attic where I found these. I think she stayed there during theater performances. Nobody knew about her, or they might stop coming to see Josephine."

"Because she was a young mother."

I nodded. "The moment they'd find out she was a mom, they might stop coming to see her show, and that would be the end of business."

"This is incredible."

"There's more," I said, letting out another shaky breath. "I have no way of proving this other than a few burn marks, but I don't think the theater burned down from an electrical fire after a hurricane, like Sid says. I think it was arson."

I thought Lily's head might explode with all this information. "Really…"

"Yes. I saw the arsonists in a dream. Callie—that's Josephine's daughter—showed me two men who were angry about Josephine's success. After all, she was…"

"Black."

"Yes. And God knows you couldn't be Black and successful in the 1920s—"

"Or even now."

"Exactly. I think they burned the theater down. I saw them do it in my dream. So, this belongs to you," I said, handing her the plans. "In case you want the historical society to assess the value, or you want to display them on the wall, or I don't know—whatever."

Lily sat, wordlessly stunned for a minute. "Thank you, Katja. I knew I could count on you. I'm going to take all this to the state, and I'm going to change my pitch a bit to include the dolls. Show this off to the execs. See what magic we can do."

"I didn't touch the oldest dolls," I clarified again. "They're at Nanette's. You don't know how relieved I am that I didn't. Sam always felt they shouldn't be altered."

"Sam's a smart kid." She closed her eyes and held the plans to her heart, a silent thank you to the universe. "I looked into it already. I didn't want to tell you, in case you didn't have them anymore, but the oldest dolls might be worth hundreds, if not, thousands of dollars…each." She reached out for a hug. "You both have good intuition."

22

The next day, I was sitting in the shade, teacups and dolls next to me, watching the house get painted a slightly darker gray than the inside, overhearing Evan talk to a contractor about a quote for rebuilding the back porch, when a familiar clunking engine rumbled behind me. My first instinct was to hide, but instead I stood, as my ex-husband rolled up, cut off the engine, and stepped out.

For whatever it was worth, I was ready for a fight.

Immediately, my entire abdomen clenched into a tight ball. Apparently, the binding ritual with his doll wrapped in SpongeBob blanket hadn't worked. Well, we couldn't solve everything with magic, could we?

"Hey." *Nahtan* was calm, collected.

From the side of the house, Evan told the contractor to hold on a minute and came storming over, ready for anything.

"What is it now?" I asked, crossing my arms to appear more in control. I signaled to Evan to stop where he was. I had to handle this on my own.

Nahtan glanced at Evan worriedly then looked back at me, shielding his eyes from the sun. "Look, I uh…" He struggled to find the words, and whatever came next, I could tell there would be a different energy attached. He carried none of the same bravado as the other day, guns blazing and making an ass of himself.

I waited.

Evan waited.

Next to me, Callie waited, arms crossed.

Yes, Callie had begun following me and manifesting herself, and most of the time, she just wanted to play, hence why I sat outside with tea and dolls. Sometimes she appeared nervous or lost, in her own world of hiding from her mother's clientele, but she never spoke with words, and was always sweet and respectful.

"Playing with dolls, I see?" *Nahtan* tried making some sort of joke, but I wasn't having it.

"What do you want?"

He hung onto the car door for comfort or safety, and made an uncomfortable "tsk" sound. "Okay, look. You're obviously happy now, and I don't want to cause any more trouble for you."

Were these words being uttered by the stubborn Nathan Miller? Inside my soul, my eyes grew wide. I could feel a weight evaporating off my shoulders. On the outside, however, I still didn't trust him and maintained my no-nonsense glare.

Not only Evan had stepped forward, but Sam had, too, standing on the edge of Nanette's property, arms crossed and giving that irritated look so many Gen Z'ers mastered. *Nahtan* was in my territory now, surrounded by *my* people. That's right—I had "people."

"Okay, so…"

"So, I'm taking off, Katja," *Nahtan* said.

I suspected he couldn't afford staying at the cheapest motel anymore, and that was why he was leaving. Even a motel in the Keys would cost him a pretty penny, but he was trying to be nice, so I didn't egg him on about it.

"But before I go, I just wanted to say…" He sucked in a deep breath and let it out in a rush. I detected actual emotion emanating from Nathan, like he used to have in the old days before he became a dick. "I know you did a lot for me, and for the girls, and for our church. I acknowledge that."

I swallowed, too shocked to say thank you.

"Because of you, Hailey and Remy went to college, a chance I never got. Yeah, I resented them for it. And you. Because Mom and Pop couldn't afford to send me, I hated the idea of sending the girls." Tears glazed over his eyes. "Figured they should work hard at a job they hate all their lives, like I had to. Maybe that's why I sabotaged them going every chance I got."

I cleared my throat. "Okay…"

He shook his head. "It's not okay. I'm sorry. I've been an asshole. I don't know what's wrong with me, but I know I have a lot of thinking to do."

"Luckily, it's a long drive back," I said.

He held my gaze a second. Then, he reached into the car, stretched across the seat and got something from the passenger seat. For a split second in time, my heart plummeted with doubt. But all he did was pull out a manila envelope. "I had these faxed this morning from the motel."

"What is it?"

"The divorce papers. I don't expect you to give me another chance, so I've signed them." He pulled out the document and flipped through the pages. "You'll see here on page ten that I'm signing half the house over to you."

My jaw dropped to the ground where an iguana now stood, watching the scene unfold. "Why would you do that? That's your grandmother's house."

"It's only fair. You're the one who made that house a home. You raised our girls. I did nothing but ruin our marriage." He inhaled a deep breath, to keep from losing it, I knew, and stared off down the street. "And because of that, I lost you."

I was keenly aware that we weren't a few anymore. In my peripheral vision were Heloise, Jeanine, and Lily, who must've heard that *Nahtan* was here and ran over from the next street, now out of breath and looking pride-like in their sisterly protectiveness.

I looked back at Nathan. Yes, he could have his name back. "That's not true. You paid bills. You were a good dad. I got to be a stay-at-home mom."

"But you didn't want that." His face turned beet red, as his lips pressed into a thin line, but he tapped the car door and slithered back into the driver's seat before I could say anything.

I let my arms drop to my sides. So, this was it. He was leaving, and these would be our last words until the next meeting—graduations, weddings, baby showers from now on. God willing.

"Anyway, I'll be waiting for those back." He looked like he wanted to add any number of extra thoughts, any last-minute words to win me back, possibly add "I love you," but he just nodded. "Take care, Katja." He gave me a last lingering look, then started the car and drove off.

I shook all over, holding onto the papers. What was I supposed to feel? Relief? Amazement? Sadness? Check. Check. Check. A mixture of melancholy that we'd failed as a couple, happiness that he hadn't caused any more harm, and it was over? Check, check. Dizzy from the heat, I turned to face my friends. "I guess that's it." I wiped away tears. "It's done. I officially have nowhere to go."

Everyone rushed me. Lily held out her arms and enfolded me in them. "Oh, honey. You'll always have a home here with us."

A week later, I lounged on a cushioned bench at the front of Jax's boat, *Sea Witch*. In eight weeks, I'd been so busy, I hadn't done any recreational outing, except for dinner with Evan. Granted, working at the Berry House had taken up all my time, so this was the first instance going out to see the islands.

"It's paradise," I said and meant it. Those who lived here had no idea how lucky they were, or maybe they did.

Lily pushed designer sunglasses down over her eyes. "Isn't it? We come out here at least once a day, even if it's just for a quick ride. I never knew how much I loved the ocean living in Long Island."

"Well, a tropical island anyway," Jax said.

"Right," Lily said.

"That's so great that you found a new home." I leaned back on the seat and soaked in the last of the dying summer's rays. "Which you never would've done if you hadn't taken your mom's suggestion to get away."

Lily's skin had turned the color of bronzed peaches over the summer. She nodded. "True. A comfort zone is a nice place, but nothing ever grows there."

"Nice."

"Thanks, my friend Terri Ann told me that once."

"She's smart."

"She is." Lily lay back against the slope of the boat's fiberglass, as we breezed around the shallow waters. "The owners were upset, by the way."

"About the dolls?"

"Yep. But as they say, 'Too bad, so sad.' They took too long to mention it."

"You snooze, you lose?" I cringed.

"That's another good one."

"Are they going to make a big stink about it?"

"Mrs. Fletcher wants to take me to court over contract wording, but she'll never win. The seller agreement clearly states that whatever the previous owners leave behind, they lose. I made sure it read that way before I bought a house full of junk."

"Crap, I'm so sorry. Like you need more to deal with."

"It's okay." She cupped her hand over her mouth, mock-whispering. "I may or may not have made an effigy of her and done a similar binding spell last night."

"You didn't." I smiled.

"I said I may or may not have." Lily returned my smile, glancing back at Jax at the wheel, pretending to be engrossed with the mangroves surrounding us instead of totally eavesdropping.

He caught me looking at him and winked. "I hear nothing. I speak nothing."

Lily laughed. "A witch's perfect mate."

Aww, those two were so adorable. I wondered if I would ever find love again in my post-divorce life. Last night, I'd felt so down about Nathan's remorseful words, the fact that I'd be leaving tomorrow, and post-project depression that I'd drank a whole bottle of wine. Then I'd phoned Evan to invite him over, and he took one listen to my voice and turned me down on account of being inebriated.

"I'll come if you need protection, Kat, but I'd rather wait on the sexytimes until you're coherent." At least he'd laughed about it and stayed on the phone with me for a few hours, and I didn't feel guilty this morning about having asked.

It was just what friends with benefits did, and I respected Evan more for it.

"Kat, there's another reason I brought you on the boat, besides you needing a break and to thank you for all the hard work you've done." Lily uncrossed and crossed her legs in my direction.

"Oh?"

"You can say no, of course, but I was wondering if you'd be interested in making more dolls for me." Her face tilted in question, and I could see my confused face in the reflection of her shades.

"Oh, uh…I don't have a sewing machine in Melville." Tomorrow I'd be on a flight back home. The girls had decided not to go on the girls' trip with their friends and were using the money to grab a flight home instead. They wanted to see me, they said, which made me cry. Of course, it did. Everything made me cry.

"I'll get you one. A good one," Lily said.

"How many do you need?"

"A lot. Enough to fill a whole theater." She flashed her pretty, mischievous smile.

"What do you mean?" My brain baking underneath the August Florida sun obviously wasn't helping.

She sat up, tanned legs tucked underneath her. "I'm going to build the theater. I've already decided." Her eyebrows wiggled.

"Josephine's theater?"

She nodded. "Uh, huh. Right where it used to be. I'm also going to be adding a new wing to the house with new bedrooms and a connecting walkway between the two *Dead & Breakfast*s."

"Whoa, you've thought this all out," I said.

Lily glanced at Jax. "We spent all night talking about it."

"So, I'd make them at home then ship them to you? I mean, sure, I would love to do that." I wouldn't have to go back to work at *Bill's Pharmacy*. I could make dolls, maybe get that Etsy store going, and Lily could be my first customer! But how would making dolls work with Sam in Skeleton Key?

This gorgeous woman pushed her sunglasses over her nose, so I could see her eyes, and took my hands. "Would you like to stay here?"

"Beg-a-pardon?"

She giggled from the excitement of her request. "Yes, here. Skeleton Key. The Berry House. You don't mind that it's haunted, and the spirits like you, which is important. They don't just like anyone, do they?"

"I…" Was at a total loss. "But the girls are expecting me," I said stupidly.

Lily laughed. "Not right now, silly. Go home, close out your estate, sell your house, rent it, whatever you want. But come back in, let's say, three or four months? Sooner if you need it. Just…stay with us, Katja." There was real hope and pleading in her voice. "You can live in the new wing."

"I don't know what to say."

"The girls can come visit anytime they want, you can make dolls in the sewing room I plan to build—"

"Wait, sewing room?"

She nodded. "Yes, I adore your dollhouse idea, and I'd much rather you make them than me hire someone new that I'm not sure I can trust. And when you're not making dolls, well…you can help me manage the new *Dead & Breakfast*!" Lily reminded me of a kid at an ice cream shop, brimming with excitement over getting sprinkles *and* crushed cookies.

I nearly fell into the waters populated by man-tickling dolphins and seahorses. "But I don't know how to manage a hotel." I could've slapped myself. Fine, I still had a few things to learn.

"Kat, Kat…" Jax shook his head. We were moving under a bridge, so Jax's voice reverberated against the pilings, like *Kat, Kat, Kat, Kat, Kat, Kat….Kat, Kat….*

Lily gave me her signature chastising look with the arched eyebrow. Thank the universe for patient friends. "You didn't know how to design or how to work for TV people either, remember? Yet you accepted the challenge, stepped up to the plate, and knocked it out of the park."

"I guess I did, yeah." That had been pretty darn bold of me, hadn't it? To apply for a job I had zero qualifications for. Pretty ballsy. "Say yes first, figure out how later," I said.

"Exactly." Lily patted my knee. "The universe will figure the rest out! But listen, you found me valuable plans and artifacts in a very historic home, items bound to be appraised for a large amount of money, and I'm grateful."

"I'm grateful, too! When would I start?"

She smiled and shook, bursting with excitement. "Whenever you're ready. I have a lot to do on my end, get plans drawn up, get them approved, get items appraised, see about getting the house officially turned into a historic location in the state…"

She went down her laundry list of to-do items, while I sat there thinking, *WHAT IS MY LIFE?* I was getting chauffeured around a gorgeous island on a boat, surrounded by immeasurable beauty with a celebrity chef offering me a full-time job. Sure, I'd lost my marriage, but it hadn't been a good one anyway. Maybe God had done me a favor by sending the masked woman to my bed. Maybe one day I'd meet her and thank her. The truth was, I'd needed something drastic to happen in order to push me out of my comfort zone. I was destined for greater things. I just hadn't known it yet. I didn't have to live vicariously through my daughters anymore. I was leading *them* by example.

Things happened for a reason.

Life was still beginning.

"If they do like the pitch," I said about the execs arriving this afternoon to meet with Lily, "How on Earth are you going to host two different shows? You're so busy as is."

"I won't be." By her smile, Lily "Fucking" Autumn had more tricks up her sleeveless bikini coverup. I could tell. She took the lengths of my overlong, dried-out frizzled hair and swung it over my shoulder. And I never, in a million years, will ever forget what she said next— words that changed my life forever. "I've been waiting two years to pay my good fortune forward, Katja. I won't be hosting—*you* will."

23

"It's right there, up ahead—the one with the…"
Construction all around. Holy moly.

"The Addams Family house?" the Uber driver
snarked.

"Something like that." I stared in awe at the
Berry House, already transformed into a gothic
masterpiece gorgeous enough to rival the *Witch of Key
Lime Lane* gothic revival. How they'd gotten so much
done already in only five months was beyond me.

Five months.

During the time I'd been away, I'd been a busy
little bee back in Ohio. I'd signed the divorce papers.
Nathan showed up in court on the appointed day, and it
was all done and taken care of without hassle or hard
feelings. In fact, there was a young lady in her early 30s
sitting in the back of the courtroom who'd accompanied
him to his divorce proceedings, one he'd quickly ushered
out the door before I could introduce myself.

Glad he could move on. Did I feel guilty that I'd
bound him with a binding ritual, thus interfering with
his free will to harass me? No.

The girls came to stay the weekend before Fall semester began then again for Thanksgiving and again for all of December. They never saw their father during that time. It'd been a year since they saw him, but according to Hailey, she was ready to face him again, only because he'd let me go in the Keys without further incident. Remy wasn't so sure, but we spent a whole afternoon making cranberry cheesecake talking about forgiveness.

Her father wasn't perfect. Neither was I, and neither was she, nor her sister, nor anyone in this world, and maybe, just maybe, Nathan might have his own new beginning and become a better man, and in turn, a better father. One could hope, right? We all deserved second chances—even Nathan.

I emptied the house of all my belongings, sold the dining set, sold my winter clothes except for one, good coat, gave the church one last donation before shipping several boxes containing my clothes, fabric scraps, sewing supplies, crappy laptop, and few worthwhile things to Skeleton Key.

And during these five months, I'd only texted Evan a handful of times. Before leaving last August, we'd agreed that I needed time to tie up loose ends of my life, gain that closure I desperately needed. Then, and only then, would I be in a position to even consider where, if anywhere, to go from there with him.

"I'll be here," he'd said, tapping my nose before giving me the longest hug. "Since I've been hired for more work."

I'd pulled away excitedly. "You have?" I'd been hoping Lily would hire Evan for more renovation work.

He was so, so good at what he did, and I was quite envious of his lifelong cultivated skills. "Did she talk to you about the side wing? The house extension?"

He'd nodded. "Yep. But someone else is doing that."

"Oh."

"I'm building the theater."

"WHAT!" I'd exclaimed. "That's fantastic!"

"I know, right?" His beaming face had been bright enough to light the path of the dark days to come. Just knowing I'd helped Evan reach one of his dreams as well as my own had been worth every ounce of sweat I'd perspired while cleaning up the Berry House.

Our time had ended in a long hug and one, short kiss.

Now, it was February in Skeleton Key, and for the first time in my life, I wore a sleeveless dress in the outdoors during winter. The Uber driver grabbed my bags from the trunk then handed them to me with a nod and a thanks.

I'd stood, staring at the house.

Gothic fantasy, I'd say. It was surreal how much it looked like something from a cartoon with its eggplant purple siding and its black spider web design gates. Lily had called last October to tell me the execs loved the doll-themed idea, and though they were wary about hiring a hostess with no previous experience, she assured them it would all work out. It was a reality show anyway, and I had it in me. Still, to placate them, she asked me to do a demo audition tape, which I'd never, ever done before.

For this, I had to look the part. I'd gotten a full transformation. My formerly straw-colored hair was now shoulder-length and black with a white stripe snaking from the crown through the ends. I'd learned from Remy how to put on cat-wing eyeliner and red lipstick, and I'd spent some of my newly-earned money to buy new threads for myself—a few gothic dresses and a killer set of black boots.

Looking the part, I felt more myself, more confident, and when I tapped the "record" button on my phone, someone new emerged out of me.

Maybe it'd been the spirit of Josephine helping me feel good in my own skin. Maybe it'd been the memory of Elvira, Mistress of the Dark, from my childhood, telling me I could be sexy, funny, *and* hardworking. Maybe it'd been Nana's encouragement, a voice that had gone quiet since the day Nathan announced he was leaving. Or maybe it was just me, same me, just another side of myself, coming out to play—but I nailed the audition as the dollmaker turned *Dead & Breakfast* Owner. Lily sent me back a video of her screaming with joy when she and the moon party ladies watched it together.

The first people to greet me were Jax and Sid, who were taking a tour of the construction site and just happened to see me standing by the street. Captain Jax cocked his head and bit his lip. "Wednesday Addams, that you looking morbidly hot over there?"

I stuck my tongue out at him but not before I blushed. He called me hot. "If anything, I'm Morticia, and you may issue an apology in the form of a boat ride later. How the heck are you guys?" I walked toward them until Sid's eyes lit up, slow to catch on. They both hugged me and extracted my bags out of my hands.

"Well, if it isn't Katja Miller, hostess of *Crone on Coconut Court*," Salty Sid drawled, ocean blue pirate eyes dancing in the sunlight. His baseball hat read: *Kiss My Bass* with an open-mouthed fish on a green background.

"Is that really the name? I love it!" I clapped with glee.

"I'm not too partial on it," Sid said. "Neither you nor Lily look like crones to me."

"Actually, Sid," I said, feeling confident after five months of researching the art and history of witchcraft. "Crone is a powerful word. Think of it as 'wise woman' rather than old hag, although I'd be okay with old hag at this point in my life, too. I've no one to impress but myself. I have my IDGAF card, remember?"

This time, it was Captain Jax who looked confused.

"Her I Don't Give a Fuck card," Sid had to explain.

Inside the house, I almost fell over. "Is this the same place I lived in only six months ago?" I couldn't believe it. My goodness, did TV network money make things happen quickly in the real world!

It looked like I'd walked into the lobby of a Victorian theater with lots of ornate dark oak woodwork, paneled walls lined with trim and molding, and lovely parquet floors. The kitchen had bloomed to three times the size and was now outfitted with retro style refrigerator, stove top, and a vintage-style brick pizza oven. The countertops alone were longer than the front porch at my old house. I was jealous of whoever Lily hired to cook there. The dining room looked like a séance room, complete with crystal ball, round table, and Ouija boards of all styles on the shelves of a built-in wall unit.

A new hire, a woman my age, stood there, outfitting a new coffee bar with creepy mugs, K-pods, sugar canisters, and a myriad accessories and utensils. She reminded me of myself when I'd arrived last July, tired, sad, and browbeaten, but willing to crawl out of whatever was bothering her.

I twiddled my fingers at her. She mustered up a smile.

"This is unbelievable." I gaped in awe at the house.

And then I heard it—a deep, rich, *sexy* voice. "Is that who I think it is?"

I whirled around. My favorite hot handyman came out of the living room, wearing a long-sleeved shirt, hands on jean hips, oozing happiness and tools and confidence from his entire aura. My god, Evan was a sight for sore eyes.

Jax and Sid walked away to give us space.

"Hello, handsome." I sashayed up to him. Who the heck was this courageous cougar leaping out of me? I supposed the hair and outfit helped encourage her.

"Hello, yourself. And for the record, I always had a thing for Elvira, Mistress of the Dark." He smiled that crinkly brown-eyed smile and reached out his arm. When I sank into it, it felt like coming home. I was not surprised by the immediate connection we had, as if I'd never left.

"I missed you," I admitted. It was true, and whether or not we rekindled our friendship with benefits, it was important for me that he know it.

"Missed you, too, Kat." He kissed my temple. "Come. It's not finished, but you have to see what we've done so far."

I followed him through the living room filled with tufted, velvet furniture and potted palm trees into a connecting area, a small tropically decorated lobby where the walls were literally lined with square cubbies. I gasped, doing my best not to ruin my cat wing eyeliner with tears when I saw what Evan had created there.

In each and every cubby, one of my creations from last summer sat, feet sticking out, glassy eyes reflecting spotlights from the ceiling, about forty in all, even though I'd only made four or five over the last months.

"Sam kept your legacy going while you were gone," Evan explained.

"Hope that was okay." Sam came out of a side door, carrying a couple more dolls in his arms. He wore black pants, a cute black top with lace, and a black hat over his fresh blue hair, which stuck out the bottom of the hat.

"Hey, you!" I drew him into my arms. I was so happy to see this kid. "Of course, it's okay. You were the other half of this endeavor. They're beautiful!"

While I was gone, Sam had made sure we had dolls in every color, with every style and color hair, with all different shade eyes, and all sorts of different personalities. The outfits ranged from sexy and burlesque to prim and proper Victorian to gothic, to modern and nonbinary, and I couldn't have been more pleased.

"You'll still be making more," he explained. "Lily wants dolls in every room, so we'll still need about ten to fifteen more for now. She expects we'll want to open a shop and once the show airs, begin selling more there."

I shook my head slowly side to side, taking it all in. The opportunities were endless, like floodgates of fortune had opened on me. Something about getting sucked into Lily Autumn's orbit, nothing seemed impossible. As her world grew and expanded, so did everyone within it. If that wasn't witchcraft, I didn't know what was.

When I heard the flip-flop of sandals behind me, I knew she'd arrived. "There she is!" She scooped me into a big, strong hug—the hug of a friend, not a boss. "Well? What do you think of the theater?"

"The theater?" I looked around. "It's done?"

"The auditorium is," Evan said. "So are the dress circle and upper circles, or balconies. Oh, and the orchestra pit and parts of the stage and backstage. It's small but…"

"Show her," Lily said, ushering me forward. "Wait 'til you see this, Kat."

I could've basked in the warmth coming from every pore of every person in this room, but Lily was still, and would always be, my icon and inspiration. "Thank you so much. I'm happy to be home."

"Have you practiced your lines?"

"Girl, I know them forwards, backwards, and inside out. You kidding? I'm not going to let you down. Not in a million universes."

"I know." She winked. "I have good intuition, too."

We strolled into the theater through the back, and for a flash of a moment, I thought I'd gone back in time. Through the upstairs closet, into the portal, and onto the balcony where I'd seen the men. Where I'd viewed the world through Callie's point of view. Hopefully, I'd see her again soon.

The auditorium was small, but gorgeous in every detail with fifty or so seats on the floor and another fifty or so spread throughout the balcony. The curtains were getting installed as we stood there, the rafters dripped with golden ropes, and the front of the stage was dotted by old-style limelights at three-foot intervals. If I squinted hard enough, I could see Josephine Berry smiling coyly at her audience over a large fan made of black feathers.

"Mangos in paradise, this is gorgeous." I couldn't believe it. Apparently, Lily, Evan, and Sam loved it, too, because they beamed proudly, reveling in my reaction, while I took it all in. "Who would have known a year ago that this would be here? All because a witchy woman we all know decided to buy another decrepit old house on the beach." I elbowed Lily in the arm.

"All because a witchy woman we all know decided to take a chance on herself," she replied. Okay, that made me cry.

"Stop, I worked too hard on this eyeliner."

"Which looks amazing, by the way. All of you does," Lily said, twirling me around to get a whole look at me. This taping is going to go so well.

Behind her, Evan nodded, eyes wide in mesmerized agreement. I would definitely have to get with that man later and compliment him on a job well done.

For the first time in forever, I felt gorgeous. Not because people were being nice, or because I'd gone to the salon, but because I was. It wasn't the hair, or the eyeliner, or the dress. Or the fact that I'd lost thirty pounds—it was something that radiated from inside of me. I loved who I was becoming. I'd worked hard to transform, but I still had more work to do, and that was part of the process.

"The theater won't be open until the end of the new show's first season," Lily explained. "The plan is to run the *Dead & Breakfast* first, offer showings to the guests staying here at the main house, then eventually open to the community. Music concerts, plays, classic movies on weeknights… We're still working out the details."

"So, when the show starts taping…" I prompted.

"The theater will still be closed. The show will follow you as the manager of a bed-and-breakfast who makes dolls on the side and dreams of running a community theater."

"Wow. I love it."

Better than feeling gorgeous, I felt successful. I wasn't a failure for being a stay-at-home mom, for dedicating twenty-two years to my family instead of working on myself. Some people worked on their careers first, families second. I'd just happened to start the other way around, and now it was my turn. Personally, I preferred it this way.

"Want to give the intro a shot?" Lily asked.

Oh, God. Not in front of everyone.

Yes, in front of everyone, someone said.

Nana? I had to do it now. The sooner I started getting comfortable with performing in front of others, the better. Besides, I'd practiced it a hundred times in front of the old, cracked mirror back home. I was ready. "Let's do it."

Lily led us all outside to the front porch. This was how it'd been done with the first show, too, and they voted to keep the intro the same for uniformity. I liked it because it felt like I was carrying on an established tradition.

"The camera will be here," Lily stood at the bottom of the stairs. Next to her, Sam and Evan watched gleefully. Soon, in about a month, there'd be crew members, too, plus Kevin, the director, plus Heloise and Jeanine, plus Nanette, and I would definitely be getting Hailey and Remy to fly out. "Now, when I say 'rolling, in 3…2…' and I go silent, you wait one second then start your intro. Ready?"

"As ready as I'll ever be."

"Oh, and after you say your line, you pick up that sign right there…"

"This one?" Next to me on a crisp, new wicker black veranda chair with orange cushion was a wooden sign, facing down. "Is this…"

"The new sign, yes. You'll hang it just like I did at the start of *Witch*. Remember? Guys, can one of you take a pic?" she asked, as both Evan and Sam took out their phones.

I nodded, fear thawing away, replaced by excitement. Within a second, my new life would begin, though one might argue it began the moment I sent that email applying for the position of temporary assistant. So many moons ago. Or maybe before that, when I went through my trauma. Or the day I first landed in Miami and Captain Jax picked me up at the airport.

But one thing was for sure, I couldn't have known what life would have in store for me then. I had to walk through the storm to see the rainbow on the other side.

"And rolling...in 3...2..." Lily pointed at me, giddiness in her smile.

The one was silent.

"Hi, I'm Katja Miller, manager and dollmaker here at this beautiful old-world bed-and-breakfast on Skeleton Key in the Florida Keys, and this is my story."

Nailed it.

"The sign," Lily reminded me.

"Oh. Right." Turning to the wicker chair, I lifted the wooden sign and shrieked with delight when I saw it. I knew Josephine would be proud of it. Callie, too. But mostly, *I* was proud. Because it'd been my idea to begin with. And because dreams and witches—they do come true.great pride and joy, I hung my new, hand-painted sign...

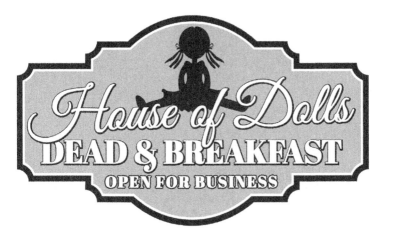

EASY COCONUT CREAM PIE

1 cup	sweetened flaked coconut
3 cups	half-and-half
2	eggs, beaten
3/4 cup	white, granulated sugar
1/2 cup	all-purpose flour
1/4 tsp.	salt
1 tsp.	vanilla extract
1 (9-inch)	pie shell, baked
1 cup	frozen whipped topping, thawed

1. Preheat oven to 350 degrees F (175 degrees C).

2. Spread the coconut on a baking sheet and bake it,
   stirring occasionally until golden brown, about 5 minutes.

3. In a medium saucepan, combine the half-and-half, eggs,
   sugar, flour and salt and mix well. Bring to a boil over low
   heat, stirring occasionally. Cook, stirring constantly, for 2
   minutes more. Remove the pan from the heat, and stir in
   3/4 cup of the toasted coconut and the vanilla extract.
   Reserve the remaining coconut to top the pie.

4. Pour the filling into the pie shell and chill until firm, about
   4 hours.

5. Top with whipped topping and with the reserved
   coconut.

ENJOY!
- Gabrielle Keyes

GABRIELLE KEYES

Book #3 in the **Dead & Breakfast Series**

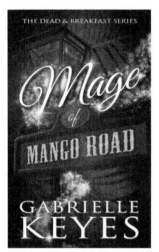

A middle-aged widow haunted by loss. A crumbling cottage on the beach. The island witches who take her in.

Regina Serra lost her son, husband, and now sense of purpose. Her grown children lead their own lives, her late husband's legacy of mediocrity weighs her down, and she's back to cleaning houses for the privileged.

This time, it's for Lily Autumn, the owner of a witchy resort in the Florida Keys, an island chain Regina always swore she'd never return to. Having fled communist Cuba as a child, northward meant success—southward meant back towards the place she left behind. A job in the Keys feels like a slap in the face, but it pays well, Lily and her eccentric neighbors are kind to her, and she gets to live in a beautiful old house.

But the crumbling Victorian is a haunted place where cigar smoke still lingers in the halls, a woman in a nightgown leaves her flowers, and a capuchin monkey appears when she least expects it. The house reminds Regina of wealth she could only dream of. With the help of the resort's staff, the island's watchdog fisherman, and a hotter-than-hell ice cream vendor for a neighbor, Regina knows the only way out of her pain is onward.

Can a woman riddled with fear who's used to serving others carve out a slice of happiness for herself on quirky Skeleton Key? At 47 with nowhere left to turn, Regina will soon find out.

MAGE OF MANGO ROAD, a Paranormal Women's Fiction novel about starting over in midlife, harnessing the magic within, and love and friendships after loss, is Book #3 in the Dead & Breakfast series by Gabrielle Keyes.

Dear Reader,

If you enjoyed Crone of Coconut Court, please:

➢ leave a rating/review on Amazon and Goodreads

➢ **join my** READER GROUP to receive *ONE FREE MAGIC SPELL* each month, new release updates, free chapters, and giveaways!

➢ pre-order Book 3, MAGE OF MANGO ROAD

Thank you so much for your support!

- Gabrielle Keyes

GABRIELLE KEYES

GABRIELLE KEYES is the Paranormal Women's Fiction pen name of Gaby Triana, bestselling author of 20 novels for teens and adults, including the Haunted Florida series (*Island of Bones, River of Ghosts, City of Spells*), *Wake the Hollow, Cakespell, Summer of Yesterday,* and *Paradise Island: A Sam and Colby Story.* She's a short story contributor in *Don't Turn Out the Lights: A Tribute Anthology to Alvin Schwartz's Scary Stories to Tell in the Dark,* a flash fiction contributor in *Weird Tales Magazine* Issue #365, and the host of a YouTube channel called *The Witch Haunt.*

Published with HarperCollins, Simon & Schuster, Permuted Press, and Entangled, Gaby writes about witchy powers, ghosts, haunted places, and abandoned locations. She's ghostwritten 50+ novels for bestselling authors, and her books have won IRA Teen Choice, ALA Best Paperback, and Hispanic Magazine's Good Reads Awards. She lives in Miami with her family and a gaggle of four-legged aliens, including the real-life Bowie.

Facebook: @GabrielleKeyesBooks
Instagram: @GabrielleKeyesBooks

Gabrielle Keyes Website:
https://gabytriana.wixsite.com/gabrielle-keyes

CRONE OF COCONUT COURT

More Books by Gabrielle Keyes

WITCH OF KEY LIME LANE
CRONE OF COCONUT COURT
MAGE OF MANGO ROAD

Books by Gaby Triana

MOON CHILD
PARADISE ISLAND: A Sam & Colby Story
ISLAND OF BONES
RIVER OF GHOSTS
CITY OF SPELLS
CAKESPELL
WAKE THE HOLLOW
SUMMER OF YESTERDAY
RIDING THE UNIVERSE
THE TEMPTRESS FOUR
CUBANITA
BACKSTAGE PASS

GABRIELLE KEYES

Printed in Great Britain
by Amazon

84355940R00139